DAYTONA BEACH DIRECTORY OF COVENS

KEVIN A DAVIS

Inkd Publishing

For April
Always

DAYTONA BEACH
DIRECTORY OF COVENS

CONTENTS

Reverend Clemens was sweating as he prepared the sacrament. Cool air blew from behind, but he stood on the balcony, facing the sun rising over the ocean and more than a hundred cars parked in front of the drive-in church. Salt wafted in the breeze. It was mid-May, and the Florida heat would only get worse with summer ahead of them. He'd grown up in Daytona, though, and he only had to stand in the full robes once a week.

He frowned as the engine of a Prius started, charging the battery of a hybrid so the occupants could enjoy their air conditioning. There was always someone.

"As we gather here around the table of our Lord, we do so with gratitude." When the choir in the room behind him stirred with murmurs, he faltered but tried to keep his expression calm for the video camera. Clearing his throat loudly, he closed his eyes, letting the sun warm his lids. He hoped the expression relayed a connection with God and not his irritation.

Furniture crashed behind him in the choir room, and he fought his facial muscles trying to snarl.

"Christ almighty!" The outcry from one of the choir was not in anger, but pure panic.

The reader to Clemens's left was already craning about to investigate, as was Reverend Danielle. He, however, maintained his composure.

Danielle screamed, and the choir joined her.

Clemens turned as she pressed her back against the railing, obviously concerned about the mayhem in the choir room. He dropped his sacrament.

The devil's own spawn thrashed into the choir chairs, abandoned as the singers fled. Grayed, skinless flesh covered the demon. Its eyes were pits of hell glowing with dim embers. It towered in the havoc of toppled chairs, stands, and music sheets. Teeth bared above raw lips of flesh, it focused on Clemens.

Screaming, Clemens backed into his display of sacraments, sending it off their second-story porch.

In a surprisingly brave move, the reader jumped into the choir room and tossed himself into the devil-spawn. A backhand slapped the man into the glass doors, shattering them and leaving the reader slumped on the floor. The vision of the demonic creature wavered as if the heat of hell rose from its body.

Clemens screamed what was supposed to be "The Lord protect," but it was a garbled screech.

The creature raced for him without having to lean down for the opening despite its height. Short black claws raked against Clemens's chest, digging through the robes to find flesh. A second fist stabbed nails into his stomach and dug deep, though the pain seemed duller than the first swipe. Still, so much of him was spilling out under his robes. It wasn't right.

Danielle fled, and Clemens didn't blame her.

The ceiling spun overhead as Clemens rolled back-first over the railing.

His congregation remained in their cars, now upside-down to him. He didn't fight as he rolled over. God would protect him. Clemens had hoped it would be later, not today.

His slide off the short piece of roof was surreal as his arms flopped and legs caught and bent. Pieces of his robe snagged, and his insides slopped around his hips. When he hit the ground on his side, the demon landed beside him, grunting and appearing to shimmer.

He watched the evil demon jog, perhaps limping, toward the palms and the adjoining woods. The world around Clemens was dimming. Doors were opening and someone was yelling, but the sounds were distant and indistinct. His lips moved, but his plea to God was silent.

I crouched beside the heavy chalice that lay on the grass below the balcony. The sour scent of wine mixed with tangy blood had stained a large area of the ground. "Do you think this is real gold?"

David, strikingly handsome even as he frowned, stared up at the tilted cross on the front of the drive-in church. "Do you get it, Kristen? I never understood putting the symbol of a wandering church on a building." He'd told me vampires weren't bothered by religious symbols, unless they harbored their own guilt. David had no guilt over religion and had attested to being an atheist when he'd been turned.

Sighing, I stood before sidling over to the next crime scene marker and continuing my train of thought. "If the witnesses are describing a draugr, then why did it leave? They tend to protect treasure, right?"

According to reports, the attacker jumped after the pastor fell, then ran north into the sparse woods. The ground around the marker was plain except for an indentation. "Is that a boot heel?" The indent appeared too sharp to be barefoot, and nothing else around the marker seemed important. Blood had sprayed from the pastor, but the CSI team hadn't marked the spatters.

In one of his usual expensive dark suits, David leaned over to search where I pointed. "Maybe." He smirked. "Maybe contamination from everyone *flocking* over before the police sealed off the area?"

I groaned appreciatively and took a few steps toward the trees. The grass was thick, with little opportunity for more than general tracks of the cryptid's trail to show. It was after one in the afternoon, a good four hours after the attack, and the area had been well trampled by the helpful congregation; still, I wandered toward the trees studying the assumed path. Nothing hit dirt to create a distinct shape.

David jogged two steps to catch up with me. "You don't think it was a draugr?"

I hadn't come to that conclusion, though the flash of video from the camera had given my team a clear indication it was a draugr. "I don't have anything to dispute it was."

When Marie, our dragon-shifter boss, came back on comms, I jumped. "We're missing a singer. They think one of the parishioners took her to the hospital because of heart pains. I don't believe she'll have witnessed more than the rest of the choir, so it can wait. Entry is still questionable from the front. Anything outside?"

"Is there gold inside?" I peered up at the balcony smeared with blood, the shattered glass door, and the opening to the choir room where her team had been investigating.

Marie was quiet for a moment before Leah, my werewolf teammate, answered, "Yes. A couple pieces. You think a draugr would have stuck around?"

"Yeah. From what little I know." Even with a little downtime to pursue my cold case and Tomas's database, I had far less experience than everyone else on the team. "What do you guys think?"

I sort of expected Finn or Tomas to chime in from the offices in Atlanta, but it was Marie who spoke up. "That is odd, but not unheard of. Can you track it?"

If Finn, the other witch in the DRC, were here, Marie would have expected him to use a dangerous spell to do so. I didn't have, or want, that ability with the Ya Keya realm and could only use my eyes. "That's what we were doing."

"Okay. Leah and I will begin canvassing the houses to the north, so let me know what you get, and we'll meet back at the vehicle."

There had been no further reports of a draugr running loose in Daytona, which seemed odd considering the time of morning. Even on a Sunday, people were out walking dogs and driving.

Local police had already canvassed houses before Finn had been notified and replaced them with the local FBI to secure the scene for us. One of the FBI was stationed at a building to our right.

The structure had been cleared, but I itched to go through it myself. My time as a lead detective had not taught me to delegate or trust someone else's search. I focused on the grass turned weeds ahead, where there was still a chance of catching a piece of dirt. Birds shifted trees and scolded us as we got closer.

David grimaced at the mix of dead and rising weeds. "Marie, are you sure you wouldn't rather have me doing the door-to-door? Leah's better suited for romping in the wilderness."

"Move it." Marie's response held a hint of humor, if you knew what to listen for.

The woods were dense with spring growth, and it took no time at all for both me and David to lose the trail. Clouds drifted overhead, but that didn't ease the heat and certainly not the bugs. Marie had already reached her first house and questioned the tenants while on the comms. The people hadn't seen anything but the commotion next door.

I circled us back a few times before giving up and pointing west to the closest house visible. "We lost the trail, Marie. You'll need dogs at this point, or at least someone who's better at this than us." With her sense of smell, Leah *would* have been a better choice.

"I think I just got a tear in my jacket." David shuffled slightly, trying to view the side of his coat. "Will you check?"

I kept focused on the way out and the bramble in front of me. "Leah, did you scent the draugr from the scene?"

"It was there, but a little faint, maybe off. Normal humans get stinky when they're afraid, and it was spicy up in that little room. Hard for me to be sure."

Frowning, I pushed through the last of the heavy brush and strolled through tall grass toward the back of a single-story house. Did I really believe someone faked a draugr?

Our canvas of half a dozen houses took over an hour, cutting through yards after Marie and Leah spoke with residents who had seen nothing. Light searches of the woods and backyards didn't yield any suspicious tracks. The houses they focused on were within sight of the woods, and half were on the dead ends of roads.

I walked away from the last house shaking my head. "Maybe it hasn't exited the woods." We'd wandered into the brush assuming the cryptid had continued elsewhere.

"Check it out," Marie said over the comms. "We're on

our way back to the choir room. Leah's going to see if she can get any better scents."

David shoved me lightly. "Thanks, partner." He pulled his jacket around to show me the rip.

We were on the northeast side of the woods and could see fairly well into it. "Really, there's only one cluster of heavy bushes. I can get close enough to check it by Haven without diving in again."

I led the way through the grass, and he followed a few steps back, grumbling for effect. Gauging the depth, I dipped my fingers into the white mist of the Haven realm and tossed a pinch deep into the woods. Life lit up white with the detection spell and showed pockets of birds, scurrying rodents, a coiled snake, a nest of possums or skunks, and a cat watching them from the grass three yards away. The birds complained loudly.

"I'm going to have to move farther west to get that section of it."

David stood ten paces away in the shorter grass. "I've got your back." As fast as he could move, I believed it.

It took three more probes with life-detection from Haven before I was sure that no cryptid hid there. The number of snakes I found made me consider switching to tall boots in the future.

In the mid-afternoon we were no closer to finding the cryptid or how it got out of Tarus. We met at the black Bronco on loan from the local FBI. I'd have to grab a protein bar from my go bag in lieu of lunch.

Slacks covered in burrs and seedpods, I spent the ride making calls in search of the missing choir member, cleaning just the top front half of my pants. Beside me, while Marie swerved down the streets of Daytona and over the intracoastal waterway, Leah touched up her makeup with a smirk. Her lavender-rose jacket and pants were markedly clear of any vegetation.

We found the choir member, a woman in her fifties, sedated and left in an emergency bed behind curtains. Marie's questions brought out nothing new and prompted another panic attack. The case was beginning to cool, and we all felt it.

"Kristen, what do you got?" Marie asked as we piled into the warm Bronco.

"Well, how does a draugr disappear? A revenant I'd understand. Could we be dealing with someone able to control them?"

"You're thinking about the ambush." Marie sped through the parking lot toward the main road outside the hospital. "You still think someone was behind the arcane user, Tim Lutwig, besides Iliodor?"

"We don't know Iliodor sent him after you." There'd actually been signs of Lutwig's split from Iliodor's causes, and his use of the Tarus realm supported the idea. "Ignoring any connection to Iliodor, Lutwig was able to control a Lich. Maybe someone is doing the same with the draugr. Otherwise, we have someone creating an illusion of a draugr."

Leah snorted. "Pretty convincing claws to gut a man on a balcony. Knocked a two-hundred-pound, thirty-year-old man across the room."

"I could do that with a moving shield out of Dur-Alf. The wounds could be ordinary knives." Knocking two hundred pounds might be a stretch.

"Keep at it," said Marie, and we twisted around a car heading for the bridge. "Leah, get ready to gear up. We're taking a walk in the woods, you and me."

David chuckled and rattled his mints. "Do Kristen and I get to stay in the air-conditioning?"

"Yes. Figure out how someone opened Tarus and got it inside. Tomas, Finn, do we have any sightings?"

"Would have let you know, Pyre." Tomas sounded annoyed in his high-pitched tone, like a petulant teenage boy.

"We're sitting on every possible communication out of Daytona, Pyre. If someone catches the cryptid on social media, we'll know in minutes. Tomas is on it. I've got every agency in three counties ready to send me an alert."

I spent an hour with David while the CSI crew worked the building and grounds. Leah traipsed and cursed in the woods as the sun dropped and shadows deepened. It was nearly dark and the CSI had cleared when Marie and Leah returned. Somehow, Leah had found coveralls and an FBI jacket to keep her clothes protected. She cocked her head in a smug smile at David while she peeled them off.

"Finn, we're going to need three rooms at least. Leah and Kristen can bunk together if needed." Marie waved us toward the Bronco.

"Four rooms across the street, Pyre. Hampton Inn. You might want to hit some food first. They have breakfast."

Smiling, I turned east toward the beach. I'd wanted to see the water while we were here, but after something to eat. David jumped to his phone so he and Leah could argue about a restaurant. She won, and we headed for a place under the bridge where I could watch water, if not the ocean yet. I'd been to Orlando with my ex, and we'd visited the ocean close to Daytona, but it had been a long while since then.

The moon was a crescent in the west when we left, and I couldn't help but plan a quick moment to check out the waves. If I were really lucky, my room would have a view of the water.

The hotel was neat, though a bit weathered from heavy use, and it took a minute for Marie to find a parking spot.

Backpack and purse on my shoulder, I waited and let the others climb into one of the small elevators. I could see the ocean from the back windows and strolled outside to smell the salty, sticky breeze. There were stairs to the beach, so I sat and dialed my daughter Jade. It wouldn't be that late in Oregon.

"Studying with Meghan." The text from Jade was short. A second popped up immediately. "I love you."

"Love you too, Honey. I'll try tomorrow."

I stared at my phone. This summer, I'd make sure to get the time to visit. Atlanta was so far away, but time was the biggest gap. It was almost a year since I'd seen my daughter. Clouds reflected the city into the water, and white caps rolled in with a soothing regularity. I sat on the beach longer than I expected.

It was just after 4 a.m. when someone pounded on my door. I'd left the balcony open for the salt air and the sound of waves. My first glance went there, then to my buzzing phone, then to the clock as I shuffled my feet out from under the covers. I'd only worn a long T-shirt.

"What?" I stumbled toward the door.

"Wheels up in fifty. We've got an issue at the office." Marie was yelling through the door.

A breeze sucked through when I cracked it open. "What happened?"

"Someone attacked Tomas and tried to get into our data. Move it." Marie glared while she spoke, then stomped away.

THREE

It was dark when I climbed aboard the DRC's small jet, an Embraer Phenom. The petroleum scent on the tarmac hinted at going home. This time I felt violated. Someone had attacked Tomas in our office, a place I considered secure and safe.

We had driven in silence and boarded without our usual banter. Marie had been fuming and deadly behind the wheel. Even David hadn't offered a quip with her mood. He appeared coiffed and smiled impishly as he took his usual seat facing the front. Marie climbed into the one beside him, and I sat opposite her.

Leah slid into the last seat across from David wearing a muted orchid skirt and jacket with shiny knee-high boots. She turned to me and chuckled for the third time that morning at my frizz ball of hair. Her straight blond hair could have been made from silk strands.

I tapped at my unruly curls, but otherwise ignored them, and risked asking Marie what was on all our minds. "What happened? When? Is Tomas alright?" Three questions came out of my mouth.

Her grimace darkened, but she didn't snap at me. "Dancing Monkeys. They restrained him and then broke into his room."

David grimaced. "Was he in the hot tub?"

"Yes. About two hours ago, so they knew his schedule. They planned it well. He was restrained with binding magic, and they tortured him to try for access. Most of his equipment is locked with biometrics. They didn't get very far, according to Finn."

"Finn stopped them?" I asked. "What was he doing downstairs that early?"

"He set up at his old desk for monitoring reports on the draugr. His supervisor office is still a bit thin on equipment."

"They didn't expect him." My eyebrows rose. "Or us, because we'd be on a case. This Daytona attack *was* a ruse." Someone had killed a pastor just to draw us away from the office. "That was an illusion, not a draugr."

Marie swore and dug out her comms, then shoved it in her ear. "I think you're right."

The jet taxied across the tarmac, and we all hurried to get our comms. Despite David and Leah's attempted nonchalance, they had been ready in a flash to get back to Tomas.

"Finn, Kristen believes the Daytona attack was a manipulation to get us out of town. I don't know how good their intel was, but they might have expected that to include you. How did they gain access?"

He sounded harried. "I've just gotten access to the video feeds. Herta is here and working with Tomas."

"Is he okay?" I asked. There was still an attraction to the Merfolk tech from my side, though he treated me worse than any other member of the team.

"No. They broke a couple fingers attempting to get

him to supply access codes. They could force him through the biometrics, but he had multiple levels of security."

My stomach churned, then heat flushed up my cheeks. From the snarl on Marie's lips, she was as angry as me. "What did they want?"

"Unclear. I haven't pushed him for too much information, just what he offered. I'm trying to get descriptions." His last comment trailed as if he were hoping to get the answer for her now.

"Keep at it." The jet began its takeoff sequence, and Marie sighed. "Update when you have something."

A phone buzzed in the background at the office. "Damn. It's Widdick." Finn's comms cut off. Now that he had taken Stacey's position, he had a couple of new bosses. One was Widdick in the FBI and another in the Consociation he never named. Marie was still in charge, though.

We were half an hour into the flight when Finn came back on and had us set up for a video feed. "I didn't recognize him, but this is agent Phillip Keipper. He works on Child Exploitation. I'm sending his file."

The video showed a blond man opening a stairwell entrance. He wore a blue suit and appeared tall, at least in comparison to the two masked men he let in. They were short and wore all black down to their gloves. Their dark eyes flitted to the camera, then one sprayed paint over it.

A second scene showed them entering our office hallway and blotting out the camera there. "How did security not catch this?" I asked.

"They had a system failure shortly after Keipper arrived. They were rebooting and had locked down the perimeter. Two of them were sent to patrol the exterior."

Finn took us through each momentary video of them as they dragged a wet, naked Tomas into his own hall and room. "Stop," I said as one sprayed the tech room cameras. "Go back."

"One last peek?" David snickered, and I blushed.

"Stow it." Marie snapped a glare at David and nodded for me to continue.

"What's that, in the other guy's hand?"

The second masked man had pulled a large cell or small tablet from his vest pocket. That was all we could see before the screen blackened.

"I don't suppose they left that behind, Finn?" Marie asked.

"No. I'm working out of Tomas's room now."

I wanted to ask how he was doing under Herta's ministration, but didn't. If they'd broken his fingers, bone would take a long time to heal. "Did outside cameras track their escape?"

"Yes. Keipper's car was in the parking lot. Security was on the opposite side of the building. Luckily. These were three powerful witches. I almost went down, but I caught them by surprise and got Tomas free. Between the two of us, they still might have had the upper hand. They blasted out the window with Dur-Alf after Tomas set off the internal alarms." Finn cleared his throat. "Keipper's car was abandoned at a Dunkin' Donuts. We're bringing it in now. Widdick's a bit out of sorts over all this, but it'll be fine."

"What's the status on Tomas?" Marie's tone softened.

"Herta said not to bother her and that Udy would update me when they had news. I think she's going to recommend a transitioning."

"That's probably best."

"It'll take time."

"I'd rather he be at one hundred percent." She saw my

expression and shook her head, so I didn't pry. "Keipper's residence?"

"Six agents have it under surveillance and are awaiting us. Widdick brought in everyone to lock down the facility and gates. No consultants or civilians. All personnel, except for Keipper, are accounted for."

We'd gone through his reports. Thirteen years in the FBI and nothing to indicate why he'd betray the department.

"Iliodor?" she asked.

"I think so."

"Me too," added David.

"It's his style of distraction and deception. All witches."

I had heard them heap suspicion on Iliodor during every case, and though it did sound like a couple of his ploys, I wasn't ready to jump on that bandwagon. "If—" I paused to give emphasis on the word "—Iliodor is involved, then we need to know his target and his backup plan."

Marie nodded. "He would have a backup plan. Where are we vulnerable, Finn?"

"Other than the gaping window behind me, I think Widdick and I have the building locked down tight."

Her face tightened, and she studied me. "Keep at it."

Thirty minutes later, after we'd landed in a warm Atlanta, gotten our black Ford Explorer through hefty gate security with a vehicle and baggage search, and nearly stripped for the building guards, we chased Marie to the elevator and then to Herta's door. We left our gear in the SUV parked outside the front walkway. An agent in a suit, not a worker in cleaning coveralls, stood atop a stepladder scrubbing a camera lens.

I swallowed my apprehension and adjusted my purse as we approached Herta's room. Finn hadn't detailed the amount of torture Tomas had endured, but the timing led me to believe it had been for over an hour. The ordeal had to be excruciating.

Udy was alone in the medical room, where I had steeled myself to find a mangled Tomas. He glanced up from his tablet. "Lounge. Knock first."

Over the comms, Finn apologized. "Sorry, didn't know."

Herta met us at the door, letting us a step inside and no further. She wore an illusion of a female doctor with missing front teeth. "I don't want him disturbed. Out."

Marie didn't budge. "Update."

Herta sighed. "Tomas is fine. He's transitioning back from Mer. It isn't as quick for Merfolk as it is for dwarves." She gestured to the hot tub.

Relief washed over me like a cool flood. There were dried stains of water across the floor from when he'd been bound and dragged out. I could see the bubbling top layer of the hot tub, and nothing more.

David sniffed and raised his eyebrows. I wasn't trying to peek.

"Once he's complete, he'll be better than new. It's a nice perk to being from Mer." Herta shooed us with both hands with an unnatural angle to the wrists. "Go. Out."

When we entered the breezy tech room, Finn's dreads bounced as he turned to give us a quick nod before returning to three active monitors. A scent of fried electrical components had me scanning for the three monitors that had been damaged nearest the outer wall. The air conditioning fought against the incoming warm air.

The window had been reduced to crumbled shards in the casing. If I hadn't known or felt the outside air, I wouldn't have noticed the missing panes. Well, aside from the pieces of glass on the floor.

"I'm no closer to figuring out what they were after, Pyre. Tomas might have a better idea." Finn's frustration echoed in his tone.

"That's going to be a while; maybe four hours or more." She studied the room. "We'll search Keipper's apartment in the meantime."

I crunched through glass to the window. Agents were stationed in the parking lot and at the outer boundaries of the property. Directly below, shards glistened in the grass. "How did glass get inside?"

"They didn't like me trying to bind them from the window and threw crushing spells into it. Two at least."

Most of the glass was below. Had they used shields to slow their fall? One shape caught my eye, and I drew a lifting spell from a pinch of watery-blue Mer. My eyebrows rose as I pulled it up toward the window. "Marie."

Somehow they'd lost their tablet, an iPad, in their fall. If they'd been busy throwing spells at Finn, they must not have noticed. Her footsteps crunched through the debris, and she joined me, then reached out her hand. I placed the iPad in her hand and dismissed the lifting spell.

I scoffed when the screen woke without a password. There was a list of names: Rhodes, Aerillus, Wan Zhu, and Asimov.

Marie stiffened. "Iliodor."

"What do they mean?" I asked.

Salmhalla glimmered at her feet so quickly, I thought it might be a reflection from the glass there. "You three. Keipper."

David hadn't seen the screen, and his handsome face frowned. "What is it, Pyre?"

Something about the list on the tablet had her flustered. "I'll handle this. Finn's got his hands full. You three get to Keipper's and get some answers. Move it." She led the way out of Tomas's room with quick strides.

Finn cocked his head at me, and I shrugged, unsure what I should say about what I saw.

We had a clue, and Marie wasn't letting us in on the details. I trusted that she would. I followed the others. At least we had something to do; Keipper had betrayed the FBI, and we needed to find out why.

The moment David opened the door to Keipper's apartment, the reek of death wafted out.

"Wait." I gestured him back to tug at the Mer and Dur-Alf realms, searching for a ward. Then I tossed in Haven, and the only shapes I could make out were someone on the couch next door and another sitting in the apartment below us. "Clear. Smell that?"

Leah frowned. "Human corpse."

This side of the apartment stretched from the door down a long kitchen to a small living area with a corner couch, coffee table, and television. The sink held soaking dishes and an open container of leftover Chinese food. The four doors to the left were closed.

David led the way in, strolling along the kitchen counter and peeking into the leftovers. "That looks a couple of days old." He turned for one of the middle doors, and I tugged at the realms again.

Keipper's file did not put him anywhere close to the arcane, and he wasn't a witch. A second attempt at a real estate license was the extent of his online activity. He had bills and junk mail on an end table by the couch. There wasn't any real art on his walls, just a football player in a plastic frame. The television was a massive black panel covering the wall.

David opened two utility closets before trying the far door into the bedroom. The bed was made, and the only clothes on the floor were work shoes and black socks.

"Careful," I said and slipped in checking for wards. The reek was worse in the bedroom. Keipper kept a fastidiously neat room except for a plate of half-finished Chinese food on his desk in the corner. The laptop was locked on the exit slide of an online course. Two flies buzzed us.

"Leah, you must be loving this." David grinned over his shoulder.

Her face held a grimace, and she was visibly breathing through her mouth. "Let's find whoever he killed and call in a team to get rid of the body."

Finn's voice was startled over the comms. "What body?"

"We don't know," I said. "Something died in his apartment, though."

Through a walk-in closet, David reached the bathroom, which would have been the first door off the kitchen. "Didn't expect that." He smirked, knowing Finn's reaction.

"What?"

Holding my sleeve against my nose, I peered around the door frame. Flies buzzed at the intrusion. "Agent Phillip Keipper is dead. I believe has been for a day or two." I winced at my cold demeanor. He'd had a life, plans, and probably family.

Hair smeared with his own blood, Keipper sat naked in the shower stall, his clothes wadded at his feet. He'd been burned dozens of times along his lips, ears, chest, armpits, and groin. Many were deep and had bled.

I shivered, then again when I thought of Tomas. Other than sheer pain, I didn't see a cause of death for the agent. I guessed a minimum of three days.

"Tortured," I added. "That wasn't Phillip you were fighting, but some witch skilled at illusion. They needed his codes and badge for work. I bet they did a dry run on Friday." His logins had him at the building on Friday, and off Saturday and Sunday with almost everyone else.

I backed out of the bathroom, leaving David to crouch and inspect the corpse closer.

"I'll get Udy and Herta there as soon as possible. See if there's anything helpful until they get there. I don't want any of his colleagues to know. I've got to tell Widdick."

"We need the security video from the building." I hadn't noticed many except on the first floor. I breathed through my suit sleeve. "I'll try to find their management company."

Leah had returned to the bedroom and gestured to the laptop. "Online course?"

I really just wanted to leave this to Udy and Herta, but nodded with my nose in my sleeve. "Yeah."

She raised an eyebrow, and I focused on the screen. It hadn't timed out for what could be days. The program had taken the full screen, leaving no toolbar exposed. Keipper had been on a class and eating at his desk when his murderer knocked at the door or entered. "You think there might have been a camera-on requirement? Wouldn't the teacher have noticed an assault on the screen?"

"Maybe they weren't watching every student, but the school might have it recorded. It's worth a call."

Maybe the attacker had never come in this room. We needed to find out. My mouth opened, then I remembered

Tomas wouldn't be answering. I pulled out my phone and took a picture of the screen. "Finn, I'm sending a company that does online classes. If they had a camera-on requirement for Phillip's class, then they might have recorded it."

"Got it." He sounded preoccupied and unsure.

"I can dig into it when we get back, if you don't have the time."

"Okay." His response left me puzzled. I'd get a better sense face-to-face.

David joined us. "I'm guessing we don't need to go through his laptop here or dig through his drawers. He's not hiding anything."

I agreed, partly because of the stench, but mostly because the possibility of a recording excited me. We needed to get the security footage for the building as well. Udy and Herta had the equipment to investigate Phillip's apartment. Considering the level of planning that had gone into Tomas's capture, I doubted they left any fingerprints.

We waited in the hall for an FBI agent to come upstairs from surveillance. The only magic I could use to lock the door couldn't be opened by Udy or Herta. I couldn't tell if the smell had reached the hall, if we stunk now, or if I couldn't get the death of Phillip out of my nose. What would the Consociation allow his family to know?

"I'm not liking this group," said Leah. She leaned casually on the wall beside the door.

"Agreed; they hurt Tomas." In law enforcement, sometimes officers got heated over punishing. I wasn't there, but anger rose against the surface when I thought about the torture. "Agreed," I repeated. "What they did here sickens me. I just can't let that get in the way and turn into revenge."

"Not going to toss them into—" David grinned as he jabbed a thumb over his back "—like Victoria?"

I hadn't trapped Victoria, the rogue vampire, in Tarus out of revenge. I'd reacted out of self-preservation. She hadn't deserved to die that way, but she had to be stopped. "No. What do you suppose happened to her?"

David covered a shiver by scratching his neck. "Nothing good. There's a very old urban legend about one of us who still survives in there to this day." His last few words were low and ominous, as if telling a bedtime story.

"We know what happens to us," Leah said.

I snapped my head toward her. "Really, what?"

She grimaced. "Bigfoot, Yeti, kind of thing. Can't get out unless a witch opens a door, which they don't." Leah gestured to her body. "Can you imagine me covered in damned fur? I mean, I'd make it work if I had to."

An agent in a suit walked toward us, so I couldn't ask if she was pulling my leg. Another thing for me to search on Tomas's database.

We left clear instructions and traipsed around the complex, eventually finding a manager after a couple calls. Access was online, and we sent the link and passcodes back to the office. We wouldn't know when to start looking until Herta got us a time of death. It would be a grueling task of matching facial recognition to tenants and known associates. Even then, we might not have a solid lead. I had to hope the online class provided something.

It was getting close to lunch and easy to agree to stop and grab something to go from a Cuban café. Finn often had lunch with his husband, Gary, but with all that he had going on, he was happy for some black beans and rice.

"Plantains," he said with the same level of distraction as earlier.

The restaurant smelled like coffee, grease, and bread. I

stood in line with my phone in hand so that people would think I was talking on it. David was already ordering ahead and the older lady at the counter was smiling. "That's it?"

"Yeah. Wait."

I rolled my eyes. "I don't have much choice. David's ordering, then Leah."

"No. I've got the recording from the school. It's huge. I wish . . . I'll have to figure out how to view it." His voice trailed off, and I hated adding more to his plate.

"Any word from Tomas?" I asked.

"No. No, not yet. I wish." He sighed. "Okay. It's loading in a program. That doesn't make sense."

I tensed, frowning at the back of Leah's head. "What?"

"All these options. Why?"

A smile tugged at my lips, imagining him shaking his dreads at the monitor in frustration. David finished ahead of me. I'd have to ask him if he got her phone number. Leah stepped forward and requested a quick sandwich, no mayo.

"Okay, Keipper is shoveling in some kind of lo mein."

"Phillip."

"Phillip." Finn's tone softened. "Here's fast-forward. He's up. Gone. Sorry, he's not returning. There's a closet off the bedroom that goes to the bathroom. I just saw movement in there."

"That's where the body is. Can you see a face?" Leah had left, and the older woman at the counter frowned. I smiled awkwardly and gestured with the phone, not that it would help. "Cuban, extra cheese."

"What?" asked Finn.

I continued as if he hadn't said anything. "Two rice and beans, two plantains, café con leche. To go." Digging in my purse, I pulled out my wallet.

"Right. Still movement, but a thin view between the doors. I'm not going to get a face."

The woman repeated my order, and I gave her a fat tip rather than wait for change. Moving to where Leah waited, we locked eyes. Her clue wasn't paying off, yet.

Finn sounded excited. "Bingo. He just poked his head in the room and closed the door. Now, facial recognition. Was that one of the options?"

"Nice." I beamed at Leah, and she bobbed her head and yellow hair. We had a lead, assuming the attacker wasn't wearing an illusion.

The counter lady was still giving me odd looks. I shifted my coat, exposing the badge on my belt. Her eyes widened, then turned a little dreamy for David. I stifled a chuckle.

"Oh." Finn's comms shut off.

After the intrusion, all three of us straightened and snapped glances at each other. Phone in hand, I texted Finn. "ALL GOOD?"

Leah watched my phone with me. I felt like my rising heartbeat would shake it. The FBI were on high alert; nothing could happen. Iliodor's backup. Now they had *me* paranoid about a witch over a century old.

"Sorry." Finn came back on comms, and we all relaxed. "Tomas is back."

"Weeds, what do you have going on here?"

"He's not too happy I was on his computer." From Finn's voice, he was grinning.

"I'm glad you're okay, Tomas." I was.

"Save it."

My eyes widened, and Leah grimaced, but I didn't respond. He didn't have to like me, but I would appreciate common respect. Now wasn't the time to argue for it, however.

We waited as Finn explained what we had been in the

middle of. Leah got her order and checked it for mayo. Mine was a larger bag, and I sipped and winced over the creamy, sweet café con leche. I motioned from David to the counter, questioningly.

"Bistek, raw. I guess cooking less takes more time."

The aroma of beans and plantains had my stomach growling. Leah took a bite of hers and cocked her head to give it a middle rating.

While we waited for David's order, Tomas spoke over the comms. "Richard Lambert. Died in 2012."

Leah frowned slightly.

We'd probably get the same from the security footage. I wasn't about to mention it to Tomas. Finn would take care of it. We still didn't have a lead.

The counter lady hand-delivered David's order, leaving the line to grumble. Leah laughed out loud and nudged his back with her elbow. In reality, he was way older than her.

"Except he's not dead," Tomas said over the comms. Even for his high-pitched voice, he sounded surprised.

"What?" I winced at my question, not wanting another of his sharp retorts.

"I ran the image through some of our surveillance of known Iliodor covens, and he came up. SDS didn't flag it."

I didn't ask about the acronym yet; there were loads in the Consociation hierarchy. It meant we had a lead. I chanced a question. "Do we have a last known address?"

"No. He's been flagged all over the east coast, including Daytona and the town where he died. Beaufort, Georgia."

CHAPTER

FIVE

Over the comms, Finn read us details as we headed for the airport. "Richard Lambert, died at age twenty-nine. He'd be thirty-five presently. Wife Alison, thirty-three, remarried. Two children, ages thirteen and fifteen.

"Richard was a developer with his father. No connections to the arcane and not classified as a witch. No secondary connections through family, though his great-grandmother was a witch. She died before he was born.

"His death was due to stage four renal cancer. Well documented, and he was buried in a cemetery in Beaufort.

"There's nothing to indicate he would be alive, or a witch."

I was sitting in the back seat, eating my lunch, and said nothing. Pickles were always a good option on a sandwich.

Leah drove us. "We'll feel out the widow, see if she has anything suspicious we should know about."

"I'll plot out all the known connections which SDS logged."

"SDS?" I asked.

"Subversion and Delinquency Surveillance."

"Meaning?"

"They make sure people don't break the guidelines and force us to go fix it. They have a division for Iliodor alone."

I couldn't be sure they were doing a very good job, but there were a lot of witches and arcane users. "Marie?"

"Haven't heard from her. I've messaged her three times, but no answer."

It felt strange, getting on the plane without Marie, like the flight with just me and Finn when David and Marie had been broken.

"Ask forgiveness rather than permission?" David rattled mints from the front. He *had* gotten the counter lady's number.

"She can recall you if she feels I've made a bad call. My only other option was digging into the Daytona covens that Lambert visited. I've got feelers out, but it will take a while to get responses."

We had just entered the terminal when Marie came back on comms. "Everyone, my office. Tomas, are you back with us?"

"Yes, Pyre. Is someone going to fix this window?"

"Building's on lockdown. I'm not letting anyone into our offices at the present time. Iliodor will have plans within plans."

Leah sounded casual. "A couple of minutes out."

"Lunch?" Marie asked.

"Flight. I'm looping through the terminal now."

"Finn will bring me up to speed. Pick me up. Move it. Finn, keep the plane on the tarmac. We've got a guest coming in, then we're on our way."

"Where?" I asked.

"Move it."

Leah sped past airport security, and David waved at them.

When we pulled up to Marie in the FBI's parking lot, she wore her usual dark suit and a worried scowl. As she tossed her go bag in the back of the Explorer, Leah hopped out of the driver's side and left the door open for the Atlanta humidity to seep in.

We sped off without a word. I think we were all waiting for her to speak, but finally David asked, "What's up, Pyre?"

"This is beyond any of your clearance. They wanted me to only take Finn, but I assured them you could keep your damn mouths shut." She drove calmer than usual. "Rhodes is a codename for our information on Clara."

David scoffed. "Iliodor wants to tangle with Clara?"

"Stow it. He shouldn't even know the codenames on that list of files. If Rhodes was top of his list, then he's after Clara. We need to check on her and talk her into moving locations."

I glanced at Leah to see if she knew who this Clara was, but she was touching up her mascara. Maybe Finn or Tomas would send a file.

"Kristen, Leah, for your purposes, you need to know that Clara is an old witch. She has knowledge that is forbidden under Consociation guidelines and is no fan of the authority we represent. However, she does not side with Iliodor in any fashion either.

"We need to protect her and convince her that a new location is necessary. She won't be amenable to anything we propose. This won't be easy, but it is crucial. The fact that Iliodor hit our office searching for that file means he believes she's within our jurisdiction."

Leah, still focused on her mirror, asked, "An old witch. How old?"

"Not necessary for you to know. Don't ask her, either." Marie swung us into the airport terminal. "We're meeting a steward here who will accompany us on the flight. She's due to land in a few minutes."

"A steward?" I asked.

"Steward of Artifacts. They work closely with archive records and the Vault keepers."

David chuckled. "I doubt Clara would appreciate being considered an artifact."

"Stow it. Keep your humor on simmer, David. Clara has been a concern of the Consociation for a long time. She is not considered an asset, but a risk. I took this position partly because of her presence in the jurisdiction."

"Is this tied to the Viewing concerning her?" David asked in a more serious tone.

"Dammit, David. You're not supposed to know about that, let alone blab about it."

"Well *now* I know not to blab about it. So, is this tied to the Viewing?"

A chill washed over me at the mention of a Viewing. I knew the Consociation had a policy about Seers, only one of the reasons my ex had tried to cocoon Jade from witches. We all knew the shadow government recruited Seers, but after working within it, now I wanted her far from the Consociation as well.

Marie's response was sharp and terse. "We don't think so." She pulled into airport parking for the small jet terminal. "I really need you to keep wrapped, David."

"Zipped, Pyre." He rattled his mints as we pulled into a spot. "Do I know our steward?"

"Bea Williams."

"Nope. The pleasure will be all hers."

I stepped into the humid air and moved quickly for the back of our SUV. If you kept in the air conditioning,

Atlanta wasn't that bad, yet. Today felt like it would be worse than the previous days.

My mind bounced between Bea and Clara with all the information, and lack of, that Marie had dumped on us. She seemed pretty sure that Iliodor was behind all this. I had to keep it as a theory until we had some solid leads.

The mystery of a dead Lambert with no prior magical abilities who now seemed deep in the covens connected to Iliodor would have to wait. If we could protect Clara, then his situation might be a moot point and a curiosity.

Backpack on my shoulder, I was a step behind Marie as she headed for the terminal.

Our plane wasn't in its usual spot when we got to the lobby. A man in dull ground crew overalls stood near it, scrolling on his cell phone. I had paused, unsure if we should board yet, when Marie walked to the window instead of heading out.

"ETA, Tomas?"

"Four minutes, Pyre."

Leah strolled up beside me, and the gray fog of Ya Keya bloomed around her as her elbow brushed mine for a moment. "I'm imagining a librarian type with those pointed glasses and a withering glower when we whisper."

"I like that look."

She pulled back, eying me up and down. "I don't see it."

David pointed out the window. "There it is."

A jet, just larger than ours, taxied toward us. I ached to ask David how he knew this Clara and how old she was. Some witches did age very well. My grandmother, Leyna, would have if she hadn't fallen off eight years ago. I missed her. A deep well of information, she would have been someone I would have asked about this Clara.

The door to the jet opened as the landing crew rolled the stairs into position. The woman who bounced out could have been a high school cheerleader.

David scoffed. "No glasses."

Petite and close to my height, she had curly, dirty-blond hair down her back, might have weighed a hundred pounds, and wore a lime green sleeveless shirt and jean shorts. She skipped toward the door, throwing a tiny blue purse with tassels over her shoulder.

Marie headed for the door to intercept our guest.

"Oh." Our steward's eyebrows, full and a shade darker than her hair, popped up when she found Marie blocking the way. "Marie Pyre. I'm Bea." She slid past, then stopped and rose on tiptoes to peer into Marie's eyes. "Hi."

"Hello Bea, call me Marie. We should go."

Bea dropped to her heels, stepped to the middle of the lobby, and studied each of us. "Uber eats is three minutes out."

"We've got snacks on the jet — and beverages."

"Java chip Frappuccino." Bea nodded to Leah. "Love the boots."

"Leah. I expected someone — different."

Bea laughed, then shrugged and widened her eyes. "Just me." Her energy was both infectious and exhausting as she bounced on two feet to plant herself in front of David. "David McCree. I've been warned." Her smile said she was teasing.

"The rumors are all true." David took her hand and bowed with a wide grin as she laughed.

For me, Bea cocked her head and snapped her fingers, producing a faint hint of the blue Mer realm. "I've read up on some of your accomplishments. Pretty amazing." She managed to put emphasis on every syllable.

"Thanks." I wasn't sure what she knew or how much access she had to DRC reports, but I appreciated the compliment from another witch.

As Marie opened her mouth to complain, Bea slid beaded bracelets off her Apple Watch. "One minute to Uber. Be right back." She dashed down the hall to the front of the building, leaving Marie with an amused yet annoyed expression. She laughed down the hall. "Don't leave without me."

"I like her," Leah said.

"Dibs." David grinned and appropriately cringed when Leah smacked his arm.

The young man at the counter fought a smile. I just sighed and watched the flight crew lug two large white suitcases toward our jet. At least we weren't saddled with a bitter type like Belinda. The Merfolk woman we'd encountered in New Orleans made me consider Tomas and his sharp response when I'd wished him well. Later, after the stigma of the torture faded, I'd need to confront him about how he treated me. I hated confrontation, but I wasn't going to put up with it any longer.

The pieces that Marie had laid out fit, which meant we might actually be dealing with Iliodor; I couldn't dismiss the possibility as easily this time. I winced at the idea of leaving Finn and Tomas alone at the FBI building. Iliodor was known for misdirection, and plans of his that had seemed doused had reignited, surprising the Consociation he battled against. I had read his pronouncements and manifesto; his assertions had some merit, though his persistence to the detriment of his followers and methods were questionable.

"Shit, that is heaven." Bea had a way of pronouncing

"heaven" that made it sound like more syllables than it should have. She jogged down the hall, hair streaming behind, white bag pinned in the crook of her arm, and a whipped cream topped beverage attached to her lips with a red straw.

From her purse, an oversized phone slid into her hand as she landed smartly in front of Marie. "Ready?"

Wiping her hand over her shaved scalp, Marie nodded. "Very. Shall we?"

Bea jabbed her phone toward the door. "You lead, I follow." As we started to parade out, she posed with red straw in pursed lips and took a selfie.

"Finn, how are we looking in Alabama?"

"Local FBI will have a car and gear for you when you land in Demopolis, Pyre. They're en route. You'll land about 1:45 p.m. local time. Drive time is just over thirty minutes."

"Alabama?" Bea asked, juggling her load.

"Yep." Marie exited, jogging toward our jet.

Humidity hung outside, drenched with exhaust fumes and spiked with sharp petroleum. I doubted Alabama would be any cooler.

The lone ground crew stowed his cell phone and jumped to help, opening the door as a man raced to get the stairs in place for us to board. They were scrambling for us today.

Our plane felt cool as I followed David inside. He and Marie were heading for their seats when I considered our new guest. I paused, peering at the tiny fold-down seat tucked behind Marie's comfortable chair.

She caught my gaze and snorted, pointing at my usual seat. "I'd rather have that chatter behind me."

As Leah took her usual seat across from David, Bea

juggled her drink and bag with hints of baked goods aroma in one arm while typing with her thumb.

Marie gestured behind her. "Jump seat. Not the most comfortable."

David patted his leg. "Very comfortable."

Bea stopped beside me. I couldn't see her expression, but she cocked her head toward Leah. "That looks comfy."

I swore Leah almost blushed when she beamed and laughed. Though the youngest on my team, I still felt like I was the chaperone on a high school field trip.

Marie was watching my expression, so I sighed and asked her, "Little over half an hour?"

She chuckled. "Just the start of a long afternoon."

SEVEN

I still tensed during takeoff and with any little bump, so I usually kept my seatbelt on during the flight. My team didn't, and David often made coffee in the back or grabbed beverages and snacks.

Bea waited until the wheels were off the tarmac before she was up and digging in her aromatic paper bag. "Croissants or lemon ice loaf?" she asked Marie.

"Hard pass." Marie pulled out her cell phone.

I hadn't received any notifications from the office. "Will we be getting any report on Clara?" I asked.

Marie didn't look up. "No."

Bea waggled her bag at me. "Don't spoil the surprise. Lemon or croissant?"

I tugged at a curl. "Lemon, thank you." We were going into the situation blind, but the Consociation and Marie evidently believed we didn't need to know. We were already exposed to their secret; information might prepare us better.

Bea dropped to sit on Leah's knee delicately and

laughed at David's pout. "Let me guess," she said to Leah. "Croissant."

Leah chuckled so low, it sounded like a growl. "You know me already."

David got lemon loaf, a laugh, and a peck on the cheek for patting his leg.

The iced portion of the lemon loaf was best, and I readily took a light and sweet coffee to help wash down the drier bits when Bea offered beverages.

"I've always wanted to meet this team," she said, serving Marie a coffee.

"Why?" Marie placed her phone in her lap and sniffed the cup.

"Success rate and completion speed ranks you at the top. A famous dragon-shifter in charge. Unique approaches make for riveting reports. All of it." Bea was serious, though she delivered everything in her light-hearted manner.

"Riveting?" Marie scoffed.

"Surely an infamous vampire warrants a mention," said David.

Bea spun with a bounce. "He would. What team is he on?"

David grimaced and put a fist over his heart. "Ouch."

"Just kidding, darling. I never miss one of your reports." She tousled his hair.

I survived the flight better than expected, though none of the conversation touched the mysterious Clara. Bea charmed everyone as best as she could, obviously flirting with Leah and keeping David at ease with her laughter and jokes.

When we exited onto a tiny airstrip in Alabama, it was hotter than Atlanta. The two women who ran the stairs and luggage were sweating and grumbling about so many planes. I saw three other planes: one jet larger than ours that had waited for us to taxi off the runway so they could take off, and two small propeller planes far to the sides. We were the only real activity I could see.

One of the agents who met us in the parking lot wore a T-shirt with an FBI logo. Outside a group of industrial buildings across the tarmac that might have been a mill, we were in the middle of the woods. The air was fresh despite the hints of petroleum.

"Did you hear that?" David asked as he climbed in the front seat of the dark blue Durango.

"What? Birds?" I was waiting at the rear door as Bea slid into the middle next to Leah.

"Banjos."

Closing the door, I grimaced at him. "Don't pick on banjos."

Bea laughed way too loud.

Marie had no problem driving through this part of Alabama, with the only traffic consisting of slow-moving work trucks. Leah and Bea chattered about a line of clothing I'd never heard of and compared pictures on their phones.

Finn offered a short update on his Daytona search. "There are a couple of questionable covens. The SDS has monitored them, and I've got confirmation from two connections that they are reclusive and 'scary,' according to their accounts. No one knows of Lambert, though. I've had to be careful in my queries, sticking with people I know will keep it to themselves."

"Once we're done here, we'll dig around Daytona. I think we'll be stuck here a good twenty-four. It'd be nice if I'm wrong." Marie raced past fields green with spring growth. "Have you or Tomas made sense of Lambert's activities since he went from dead to witch?"

Tomas piped in, "I'm thinking he's always been a witch, Pyre. His family was deeply religious, and they had him under counseling since he was six until he headed off to community college. It fits the pattern of family denial."

I cringed. Covens usually found "orphaned" witches and approached them, but not all were open to defying their family, or they considered magic an affront to their religion.

"What, you think Iliodor got a whiff of his abilities and turned him? There's precedence." Marie passed a meandering sedan with more stickers than windows.

"Exactly, Pyre. He had to be pretty convinced to leave his family."

"Iliodor can be convincing. How much farther, David?"

"Should see it soon. Up on the left."

All I saw were trees as a little forest cropped up at the edge of the sprawling field. Birds circled the tops and dove at some intruder. There were almost no clouds, and I imagined the heat had risen during our drive. If we ended up outside, I'd be soaked in sweat.

"Are we allowed to meet Clara?" I asked.

We blew past a white fence marking an entrance. "Be difficult to avoid that," answered Marie. We drove by fenced-in utility equipment on the right and a little house down a gravel drive on the opposite side.

David pointed through the windshield to a hint of a driveway where the road rose up a low incline. "Up there. Left." Woods closed in on both sides of the road.

The metal fence had mesh tacked to it for no reason I could imagine. The gate had a wooden arch built over it. I expected a ranch symbol at the top, but it was plain; the only sign warned to keep the gate closed. Marie pulled in, gravel crunching under the tires, and turned back to study Bea.

"We just let ourselves in?"

Bea wiggled in her seat. "I'm sure she already knows we're here."

David unbuckled himself.

"Leah, get the gate. David, sit."

He spread out his hands questioningly. "What?"

As Leah slid out, letting in a wave of heat, Bea spoke sweetly. "First impressions are important."

David mocked a dour expression and a single raised eyebrow. "Clara loves me."

"Tolerates is what the report said. You met once about eighty years ago."

I imagined a curled-up woman with white hair and wrinkles deeper than the Grand Canyon, even if David had met her as a baby. The witches I'd met who lived past eighty appeared only a decade or two younger. I'd put Clara at one hundred until I knew better.

Marie pulled through the gates Leah opened, then waited for her to close them behind us. The top of a building was visible just up the slope to the left, but it might have been a barn, not a house. The driveway appeared to trail off to the right.

Leah jumped back in, and Marie crawled forward uncharacteristically slowly while she scanned the field we passed through and the bordering trees.

A pond spread out ahead of us, and the drive split to the barn with numerous out buildings on our left, and into the woods to the right, where a wood and brick house over-looked the water.

"Exciting, isn't it?" Bea asked me.

I'd been leaning forward to see through the windshield. "I guess. Maybe more so if I knew who we were meeting."

Marie grunted, but didn't tell me to stow it. I got the hint, though. I'd learn all I needed to know when she felt it necessary. If this Clara were that important and needed protection from Iliodor, then informing us could be helpful. Besides, I'd rather be investigating than babysitting a witch who didn't like the Consociation.

There were no cars parked at the house, but a trickle of smoke drifted out the chimney. Trees dotted the parking area and grew into a forest away from the pond. The wooden building had a brick foundation higher than I expected and a metal roof that pitched to a small second floor.

"Nice cabin," said David. "Quaint." He might have considered it a cabin, but I'd grown up around rural houses, and this was typical.

Flowers bloomed in whites and reds, and blue curtains hung in the windows. A face appeared to study us, and it was not what I had imagined.

"Comms off," Marie said as she snapped her seat belt loose.

CHAPTER

EIGHT

S imilar to my own, Clara had the Mediterranean shade of brown skin tone, and she appeared to be fifty at the oldest. Her eyes were dark and gave no hint of surprise or annoyance that we parked outside her house.

She watched as Maria opened her door, then disappeared from the window. I glanced at Bea, but she was already urging Leah to exit. The hot air smelled of pine and spice. My stomach growled as I opened my door.

Clara opened her door wearing a low-cut black bodysuit with a beige skirt draped down to dark knees. Gold glittered at her ears, neck, and wrists, with a twinkle of light green at her chest. Her feet were bare as she stepped out.

"I recognize two of you." She studied us quickly. "A dragon-shifter, a vampire, a werewolf, and two witches; what does the Consociation want with me?"

Bea bounced forward, hands clasped behind her back. "Steward Bea Williams. This is Marie Pyre of the Department of Realm Containment. David McCree you've met.

Kristen Winters. Leah Manson. May we seek audience regarding your safety?" Her tone was light and friendly, while maintaining an officious air.

The "old" witch in front of them lowered her eyebrows at the last part. The lightest lines formed about her eyes. She sighed, tugged on Dur-Alf, and elaborate wards between her and us popped into brown-green dust. "Come in." Her skirt flared with her quick turn, and she stepped inside.

The house was cool and smelled of incense, cedar, and grassy olive oil. The walls, ceiling, and floor were various shades of wood, and the windows to the pond were uncovered, letting in the sun. A black granite bar separated an extensive kitchen from a comfortable sitting area beside the fireplace. A black pot hung over light embers.

"What is your safety concern?" Clara asked as she motioned to the couch and chairs. She stood close to the hearth and an older black chair with its back to the pond.

Herbs hung from the upstairs loft and along the stairs. Statues of Egyptian cats carved in onyx decorated the mantle behind her. I took the couch with Leah while Marie and Bea remained standing.

"Iliodor attempted to steal your file from our secure database. He wants your location." Marie's gruff voice caused Bea to wince.

"Then get rid of the file," Clara responded quickly. "I assume, from your comment, he does not have it."

"No, he does not. It does warn us that he has grown interested in you once again. Your general location is known to him."

Bea sounded like a bird chirping beside Marie. "We just want you safe."

"Since I have done nothing to attract his unwanted attentions, then I must assume his knowledge has come through the Consociation." Clara crossed her arms. Smooth-skinned and toned, I could have believed her in her forties. "Lose the files, and I should be safe once you've forgotten where I am."

A pair of cats with sleek gray fur called from the loft balcony. We all turned, but Clara spoke to them. "It's okay, dears. Go enjoy the sun." Sitting like bookends, they flicked tails in unison before rising to disappear.

"We can't ignore the threat," Marie continued. "We'd like to discuss relocation."

Clara huffed. "I've only been on the land for a couple of decades, after your last imminent threat. I just built the house two years ago. Hunting is good. The ponds are finally fully stocked. I'll not be 'relocating' any time soon."

Bea pounced on her toes as she pleaded. "We understand all the trouble you've gone through moving to America, but you are precious to us."

"The only value you see is keeping me from Iliodor's grasp. Where's Rodney?"

Stiffening, Bea answered quietly. "Colon cancer."

"He should have come to me. It is sometimes treatable." Clara raised a hand as Marie started to speak. "I left England when the little rat began sniffing around because it had gotten so crowded around my estate. I've got over five-hundred acres here, and no one wants to move here any time soon. Leave me be."

"The Consociation can't protect you if he finds your location." Marie's statement was sharp.

"The Consociation still overreaches in every aspect; in that, Iliodor is correct." She waved off Marie's response. "I've had this argument since the beginning. I support rights for everyone and even agree that certain knowledge should be laid to rest, but enforcement of those guidelines creates new dilemmas which have not been addressed."

"There's an open seat on the Council with your name on it. Always an invitation."

"That's no life. Stuck in meetings all day, arguing semantics."

"Some have chosen to sacrifice their time for a better Earth."

Bea winced. "We are not here to bring up old debates. Our only concern is providing a safe space for you, however you would like to live it."

"Then forget about me, and Iliodor won't find me."

David had taken the seat beside our couch. "And if it's too late?" His tone was calm and not confrontational.

Clara studied him. "David McCree now? You always did like to surprise people by being smart. They always underestimated you." She nudged her chin toward Marie and us. "Probably a good place for you."

"Easy job to meet chicks." His easy grin broadened to a smile, then he grew serious. "You didn't answer my question."

"Because I don't want to think about that." She gestured to the house. "I've gotten comfortable. If it came down to it, I can't stand against him and his covens without breaking my word and using magic even I agree shouldn't be known. I'd have to leave."

"Then let's be proactive," said Marie.

"No. If I've got proof he has me, then I'll disappear on my own, and you'll all get to wonder where I am." Her expression had hardened as she lowered her gaze at Marie. "What happened? How close was he to my information?"

"He knew enough to attack my office and knew the file name. Hurt my people in the attempt, but we stopped him." Marie could have lied, and said he might have the file. I might have done as much to force Clara to safety.

Clara had her points in the argument, but she was also

being stubborn. If Jade had someone like Iliodor after her, I'd move her without packing. More and more, I had accepted that he was behind this. I would have to push that away, or I'd lose clarity on the facts we had.

Turning toward the fire, she swung the pot off the low heat. "No. I stay. Do what you need to, but until you've got proof, or he comes knocking, I'm not running."

Outside, spring grass sloped toward a pond as much green as blue. It had an artificial appearance with a host of well-spaced trees at the front and a manicured shore of grass about the water. This was a home she or the Consociation had created.

I thought of her comment about ghosting the Consociation, and this would be a good way to do so. Tell us she'd ride it out, then leave. I'd have to mention it to Marie in private.

Marie turned and glanced at me, of all the team. What did she think I could bring to the argument? "We'll have to bring in a protection detail." With a sigh, she tapped on her comms and walked toward the kitchen. "Finn, I need a protection detail dispatched here."

Leah tilted her head, and I wondered if she could hear at this distance.

"Then we stay until they arrive." Her voice was sharp with anger just under the surface. "Text me the details when you have it worked out."

Marie frowned. "Birds? Yes, let Herta do whatever helps. Keep us on lockdown. Don't let Widdick get soft." She left her comms on and turned back to us.

David chuckled. "Birds? I'm guessing Tomas's office."

"Herta's going to block it." Marie stood behind him. "Two in the car watching gate and house. Two inside."

"Leave the quiet ones. The werewolf and the witch."

Clara dropped into the strange black chair beside the fireplace.

Marie shrugged and focused on me. "Grab your gear out of the car. Comms on. It's going to be a long run. Leah, Kristen, take turns napping."

I jumped up, smiled at Clara, and headed for the door. We weren't exactly guests, but she didn't seem upset about us being in her house.

Leah sauntered behind into the sweltering afternoon heat. "Did you bring any nut bars?"

"I did." We'd skipped lunch except for peanuts and lemon loaf on the flight. Out of curiosity, I tugged at the Dur-Alf realm while I was at the car. Wards lit up the windows and walls of the house. We were probably safer inside.

Clara had moved to the kitchen while we were collecting our go bags and extra water. She pointed to a hall under the stairs. "There's a spare room there with a bed that I use to store fall herbs. You can put your belongings in there and nap if needed."

Chives or scallions simmered in butter as she sliced mushrooms. "Venison okay for dinner? Rare for the werewolf and vampire. Blackened for the dragon-shifter. Kristen? Bea? Preferences?"

"Yum," said David over the comms, and I couldn't be sure if he were joking or not.

Bea smiled in a way that told me game was not her preferred meat, so I answered first. "Medium rare. Otherwise, it gets gamey." I'd grown up in Oregon, and all the hunters had brought my mom and grandmother supplies after my father had passed.

"Same. Need help?" She recovered with a grateful expression and bounced to the edge of the kitchen.

Leah and I dropped bags in the first room. Some of

the fall herbs were still hanging in bundles on a rack to our right, but the small bed looked tidy.

I joined Bea at the sink with half a dozen potatoes. Leah took a high stool at the granite bar, loosened her Kevlar vest slightly, and watched us.

Clara caught my eye. "Who did he hurt at Pyre's facility?"

"Tomas Ellis." I answered, waiting for some sharp retort over the comms.

"I met him. Turn of this century. Off to some research in Norway with a friend of mine. Bright young man."

Grimacing, I gestured to the comms in my ear.

Her lips twitched in a devilish grin. "He's got a nice ass, don't you think?"

I choked and waited for the tirade.

David replied throatily. "Definitely."

"Stow it."

Clara's expression dropped, and her eyes were unfocused when she turned off the fire to the skillet.

Over the comms, glass shattered, metal groaned, and Marie swore.

I dropped a potato into the sink. "Marie? David?"

Clara wove wards, sending them slapping against the windows. "Go, help them. Bea, stay with me."

Leah was already heading for the door where we'd parked. I was six steps behind her when I dashed out the open door. How had they found us?

The sun had dropped into the trees to our left, shining slices of light at us. Dur-Alf bloomed from the shadows. The witches threw binding and crushing spells from there, but this close to the doorway and warded walls, Dur-Alf exploded around me.

I tried to throw a shield in front of Leah, but she moved too quickly. Her shoulders were already thickening and straining her Kevlar as she partially morphed into a wolf and dove toward the trees.

Metal still groaned far behind me, past the water, but I didn't dare turn as the four witches in the woods to the west were rapid-firing Dur-Alf at Leah and me.

A gun flash lit the shadowed green, and I flailed a wide binding spell in that direction. Sunlight stabbed my eyes as trees shifted from me or the wind. Two larger flashes fired near the gun sent missiles streaking toward the back of the house to my left. In the mere seconds since the attack, I'd barely made it three steps from the door. I was reacting rather than acting.

I whisked a shield toward the wall, but I was too late.

One fireball after the next blasted wood, glass, and air into my side. My attempted shield caught some, but Clara's Dur-Alf wards knocked me to the ground when they went off in response.

Back in the forest, shapes blurred with the Mer realm as I rolled into a tree. I coughed dust and plucked at Dur-Alf.

Two men in thick vests were racing toward the back of the house, both streaking with the blue of a Mer speed spell. I had to focus on keeping them away from Clara. My comms weren't working. Even with the ringing silence caused by the explosions, I would have picked up something.

Flicking twice, I spread weak but massive shields at the back of the house. There were gaping holes of shredded wood where windows had been. The door that I'd never gotten to close hung on one hinge. I could smell explosives and wood that smoldered in places.

As my spell hit the wall ahead of them, I smiled and readied a binding spell.

Their Dur-Alf blast, which hit the tree beside me, shattered the trunk. Splinters darted into my hair and stabbed into my neck at the Kevlar collar.

A dull ring sounded from one of the men in a thick vest. My shields and Clara's remaining Dur-Alf wards puffed into green clouds everywhere around her house.

The first blur dove into the open, and the Haven realm

exploded in white flame. The second man dove into the house as if his comrade weren't a screaming torch.

The remnants of the tree groaned as branches slid down the trunk and crashed into the ground beside me. Scrambling, I fought limbs but managed to stumble clear as the top, still fifteen feet high, toppled to the ground.

Leah, half wolf with shaggy tan hair and black claws, flew backward out of the trees with a Mer lifting spell partially wrapped around her. The Kevlar rippled loosely about her shifting torso; her skirt was shredded, and her boots were gone.

I snapped my own lifting spell to slow her. That was when I saw Lambert running out of the sun-speckled woods. His gun flashed three times, and one bullet punched me in the Kevlar.

The vest had stopped it, I hoped, but the impact folded me. More than the pain sunk in as I fought, admitting we'd been out of control of this situation since the moment they hit us. Worse, we'd played into their hands.

Even as I stumbled back, Lambert fired twice at Leah as she slapped to the ground, then he joined another man to run for Clara and the ruined house.

Ego kept me from falling, though I hadn't got my footing fully under me. I swung two Dur-Alf binding spells at the man and would have caught him but for the faint ring of crystal that turned the magic to dust.

I had to believe they had a talisman or some other arcane magic; nothing I knew could disperse Dur-Alf. My back slapped against a thin trunk. The ground sloped toward the pond, but I could still see the back of the house. Marie and David were behind me somewhere, or had been.

Lambert's eyes never wavered from the opening in the

back of the building where one of his witches still smoked from the Haven ward; his companion was already inside.

Wincing, I unsnapped my holster and drew my weapon.

A watery-blue lifting spell from Mer, two of them, flicked my gun from my hand. One slid along my body and tightened around my middle, causing me to gasp in the renewed pain.

The yank of my body in the air felt like it wrenched my insides. The world spun with daggers of light and shadow, green tree tops, and clouds in a blue sky, then grass and leaves slapped against my face. The slope was sharper than I expected, and I rolled toward marshy smelling water.

Our SUV was in the water on its side. I snuffed dirt into my nose and choked, rising on an elbow in the process. David wrenched open a door and was atop the submerged vehicle as quickly, reaching inside, I assumed to help Marie.

I curled onto my knees and turned to Clara's house. They'd shot Leah in partial werewolf form, but she'd still had on the Kevlar. The front of the house was deceptively quiet from where I'd been thrown. Under my hands, water oozed in the grass.

Pulling a knee under me, I threw a detection spell to the front door. There was still life moving inside, but no distinct shapes. As I stood, my eyes flicked to the woods where Leah had been thrown. I had to trust her werewolf durability and the Kevlar to have kept her alive.

Bea and Clara were more vulnerable. Iliodor, or whoever was behind this, wanted Clara alive. I stumbled toward the house.

Lambert poked his head around the corner of the house, bathed in the white of Haven from my spell. Expecting a gunshot, I threw a panicked shield in front of me, not knowing if it would crumble to dust like my other attempts with Dur-Alf. The spell held.

He disappeared back to the jumble of incoherent shapes in white, but he'd stalled my approach for a second. I started to run in earnest as David blurred past.

A chill crawled through the sweat under my vest. The shapes weren't in the house. Anything alive had moved deeper into the woods, so I threw a second detection spell. I couldn't warn David. My comms weren't working even as I tapped them on and off. There was only a slight click of quiet static.

Leah rose to her knees and palms in the woods, and I let out a breath of relief. She moved stiffly.

We'd failed to protect Clara. She was either dead or gone. Gritting my teeth, I found the energy to race behind David. Marie would be okay, somewhere behind me.

As I was running up the side of the house toward the corner, Dur-Alf exploded somewhere in the back. David's form, ghost white in Haven's spell, flew from the woods.

I didn't slow as I readied two spells, a shield and a binding. The other shapes in the life detection spell were faint in the woods beyond David and moving away quickly. He'd hit the ground stiff. As I turned the corner, I could make out the mossy green binding spell wrapped about him.

Stumbling, I adjusted from a full run into the woods and skidded to veer toward him. An angry expression locked on his face, he lay on his side, eyes open. His clothes were ripped, especially at his legs. Dirt covered his face, and blood welled at scrapes on his hands. Dropping beside him, I scanned the woods.

There was no sign of the attackers, not even in my Haven spell. David and Leah were the only living things larger than a rabbit.

"Hang on," I said, kneeling beside David and digging fingers into the binding spell. From the blast pattern, the ward had been set to cover their trail, blending a blast and a bind. Tricky work, and deadly.

Marie flew past me, not for the woods where I guessed Clara had been taken, but into the house where I feared Bea waited for us. She didn't know that nothing was alive inside the building. I didn't even think Clara's cats had made it.

David snarled when he was released and jumped up. His eyes flashed from me to Leah, to where Marie had entered the house. He stared longest into the woods where we'd lost the witch we were supposed to protect.

TEN

"Are you okay?" I asked David. A shiver rolled across my shoulders.

"Not at all." David stomped toward the ruined house. "They took her."

I rose, glancing back at Leah, who strode toward me, appearing to flex in and out of a partial werewolf mode. Her vest had two bullets marking her upper chest.

For the first time, I tenderly found the bullet embedded in my Kevlar. My stomach was bruised, but my curves had added some protection. It had hurt worse a minute ago. We'd been outmaneuvered and outgunned. I winced as the breeze brought the reek of smoldering flesh.

"Do you have comms?" I paused for Leah. Marie and David might find Bea and Clara inside. I'd know soon enough, and could do nothing about either of them at the moment.

She tapped her comms, then dug in her pocket for her phone. "They're blocking what little signal we had."

Blood marked Leah's left sleeve as it flopped loose at her elbow, but I saw no damage to her arm. Her face had smoothed to human, and she still had an angry grimace. "Is David okay? I couldn't warn him in time. I knew they'd dropped a ward from the way they gestured. They have Clara and Bea."

"They took Bea?" I asked hopefully. The relief was purely because she wasn't dead inside the building. In a short time, I'd grown to like her. My detection spell had started to weaken, lessening the ghostly overlay it put on her, so I turned to check on David and Marie. They were standing together, almost faded into one shape. Leah passed me to join them.

"Both her and Clara were bound stiff. Lambert was there, leading it all." Leah climbed inside and sniffed.

I winced, my stomach muscles rebelling at climbing the steps. Over the burned body, I could smell little else, especially after we entered the scorched living room, where a second blackened body wrapped over the top of the granite counter into the kitchen. A male from the body frame, his clothes had been turned to ash or melded with fatty tissue. Charred bones pressed through skin at the fingers, ribs, and face. Identification would be difficult.

Marie stood at the entrance to the hall. "Kristen, anything hiding in here?"

I refreshed Haven, just in case, then shook my head. "Nothing. I hope the cats got out."

David shook his head and nudged his head toward the upper floor. I didn't look.

"Bea and Clara are alive." Marie, drenched, still appeared in better shape than any of us. "I smell explosives that I assume they used to breach the back. Anybody hurt more than I can see?"

When we didn't note anything, she tilted her head toward our vests. "We'll get those looked at anyway. David, get to the road front and see if you can clear whatever they have suppressing comms and phones and contact Finn. I want local FBI out here and a lockdown on air traffic, local roads, everything. Move it."

"Got it, Pyre." He flashed away, leaving Leah and me with Marie and the burned corpse.

"You two probe out back and see what you can get from their trail. Did they have any vehicles?"

"No. Clara and Bea were both stiff. I think the men carrying them used lifting spells because they ran as if the women weighed nothing. Lambert was with them, setting wards. The last man covered their rear with what could have been an AR-15." Leah already moved toward the rear.

"Go slow. I know you'll be careful, Kristen."

I hesitated following Leah. "How'd they know?"

Marie snarled out her response. "I'm going to guess we led them here. We'll have Tomas go through everything we brought on the plane. They were prepared and too quick and precise to track us without pinpoint accuracy."

I started pulling at Dur-Alf, Mer, and Haven as soon as we exited and pointed out the wards I could see. Discretely, I pulled from Earth and sent a muddy waver over my bruised stomach.

As I began disarming a number of complex Dur-Alf wards, Leah hovered nearby, sniffing at the woods and glaring as the afternoon shadows lengthened.

"She uses Haven for fire, Clara does." I frowned at the two threads I tugged at simultaneously.

"I've heard it was possible. Burned pretty hot."

"Targeted too, or the house would be burning." The woven wards puffed into dust. "How'd they stop her?" I knew from a prior case that escape into Haven was a very viable option as well. "I would have assumed a team of even six would not have been enough."

"They had plenty of tricks. What did that gong do?"

"Gong?" I shifted us to the next ward, the last I could see.

"One of the men in the lead kept tapping a crystal cymbal like a gong. I assumed it did something."

"Dur-Alf was disrupted. That must have been what caused it." Without comms, I couldn't ask Tomas or Finn. "We'll have to bring it up when we're back online."

"Do you think they tracked us?" Leah asked.

I studied her before starting on the ward. "Had to." Did she suspect Bea or Clara were involved somehow?

"Pretty fast on their attack. We were there maybe an hour and a half from when we arrived at the gate to the attack on David and Marie. RPGs or whatever the missiles were, cell jammer, and a team of what, eight?"

"It is a lot to plan, but we knew Iliodor would have a backup."

"So, possible."

I turned the wards into a puff of mossy green and drew from the three realms again. "Clear ahead." The house was still easily visible, and Marie had exited. "We'll need to grab our bags." The thought that one of our belongings had been compromised made me wince.

Leah sniffed, stepping carefully forward. "There's equipment, metal and electricity, just ahead. They exited past here, so they might have rigged something or picked something up. The jammer proves they want to delay us and get some time to clear the area. One hell of a lot of prep to drop in Clara's backyard. Not that I think she's working with them."

"There would have been no point in attacking Tomas or the office."

"Whoa, stop! Trip wire. We might want one of your shields, just in case."

I tugged Dur-Alf into a half a circle shield in front of us and let Leah guide us over the wire. "It leads over to the left, then forward again."

"Saw that. It's going to that clump over there that I think is camouflaged equipment. The weapons were fired from here at least."

Out of caution, I dropped a shield right in front of the now obvious lump of vegetation. "I've got us covered up there as well."

"I'm going to take us wide. You're sure there's no wards?"

"Clear."

"It's all a bit odd," Leah said. "Clara said she'd ghost the Consociation if Iliodor got wind of her. Too late, I guess."

She had me second-guessing everything, which is good in an investigation. I didn't want to believe either Clara or Bea would have betrayed us. It seemed more likely that Lambert had planned on us going to Clara once we knew which file he was searching for. He'd left the iPad for us to find.

The netting over the discarded RPG tubes was obvious as we neared them from behind.

"There." Leah knelt and pointed to a brown plastic case hidden under the end of the RPG tube. "I wouldn't know how to disarm it."

I gestured toward a crate. "What do you think that is?"

She circled carefully. I had two layers of shields between us and the entire pile. "That's an antenna, four of them, poking out the side. Our jammer."

Netting covered it, along with loose branches. "Want me to try and open the lid?" I tugged at Mer for a delicate lifting spell.

Leah shrugged. "Hoping for an on off toggle?"

"Comms would be useful."

She studied me and laughed. "Give it a go. You can keep the shields up too?"

I nodded, took a deep breath, and trailed a delicate tendril of Mer to the lip of the jammer box. After a light tug, the lid rose about an inch before it sparked inside.

The explosion set off the mine next to it along with a couple other nasty items under the netting.

CHAPTER

ELEVEN

Comms returned in time for us to catch Marie swearing up a storm as she jogged from the house toward us. My shields had held, but dirt, leaves, and metal showered down on us. The nearby tree tilted into the hole we'd made. Sweat ran under my vest and shirt.

"We're okay, Marie," I said over the comms. "We found the jammer."

"No shit. Finn? David? Tomas?"

Finn answered. "We're here, Pyre. We were just setting up a cordon around your area with David. We already had local FBI out of Tuscaloosa heading your way. Likely, we are not going to get a very tight net around your location. Not in time."

"Cold sands." Through a rolling cloud of debris around us, we could see Marie standing at the edge of the woods.

"You want us to continue out here?" asked Leah.

Finn sighed. "No need. We know where they went, and you won't catch up on foot. Neighbor to the west reported kids on ATVs tearing up his property, probably on their way in. Local enforcement is over there now. No sign of Lambert and his team, but we're monitoring. It's going to be twenty minutes before we have air or ground support for you."

Leah paused, eyebrows arched. "Pyre?"

"Yeah, Finn's right." Marie's comms cut off.

I shook dirt out of my curls — some of it. "When was the call from the neighbor, Finn?" Leah had been right to question how this could have been so well-timed.

"Call came in at 2:44 p.m. your time. Comms went down fifty minutes later."

"Well, we got to the property around 2:30 p.m., so fourteen minutes after we arrive they're bringing their men and supplies into the neighboring woods for an attack into the rear of the house?" I glanced at Leah as we walked side-by-side. "That's pretty tight timing."

"Yeah." Finn's response was thoughtful. "It is. If they moved people and equipment in sync with your movements, they'd have to use the same rural airport. Tomas, can you check that?"

"Pulling up flights will take a few minutes." Tomas didn't add his usual reproach to his tone.

Marie was talking on her cell, drifting away from the house and us as we approached. I slowed, unsure what we were supposed to be doing now that I'd blown a hole in the woods. Our charge was being swept off by the same kidnappers who'd hurt Tomas and tortured Phillip to death. We hadn't even talked about the man, but exactly how he died wouldn't change what we were doing.

David had returned and waded to the Durango. "I might as well leave my suits," he said over the comms.

Tomas piped in quickly. "Everything you initially put

on that plane comes to me, including purses, watches. Even clothes you are wearing, eventually."

"Slightly used Kevlar vest?" asked Leah.

"No. Yes, it might have already been on the ground in Alabama, but perhaps they got our flight plan." He remained very serious, but he couldn't see Leah's smirk.

I wasn't sure how we were going to send my purse, clothes, and belongings to him, but he didn't push it with details, so I assumed we'd deal with that later.

David stood on the exposed passenger side of the SUV, peering into the submerged interior. I almost would have rather gone diving for their bags rather than go back inside Clara's house for my backpack and purse. Leah appeared as excited.

We were inside when Marie jumped back onto comms. "Finn, do you believe Lambert's base is Daytona?"

"Can't say for sure, but yes, Pyre."

I had my nose in my sleeve against the reek of the scorched man on the counter. My purse remained stuffed in the pillows of the couch. I found Bea's as well. Leah handed me my backpack as she marched out of the summer herb room. Our potatoes had been knocked to the kitchen floor, and the pan waited at the back burner. My stomach twinged as I slid the load over my shoulder.

"Until we have any other lead, we're heading to Daytona." Marie didn't sound pleased.

It was hard to consider Bea a suspect. She hadn't known the location until we'd been ready to leave the airport, and it was at that point she'd been on her phone.

Tomas piped over the comms as we were stepping out into the deep shadows of the fading afternoon. "Flight plans are in. One is promising. It originally took off before you from Fulton County Airport. Booked two days ago, then six times throughout the morning the clients adjusted flight plans, including times. Paid all the extra fees. Eight passengers and luggage. Delaware corporation named Bright Synergy with no physical office. It arrived fifteen minutes before your jet at the same airport as you."

"They knew where we were going before we took off," Marie said. She'd wandered to the edge of the water. David tossed soggy luggage to the shore.

"Marie, what if we check all calls from DeKalb to Fulton from the moment we arrived at the airport?" It was a cheap way of not feeling guilty about suspecting Bea. "Maybe check social media of anyone there as well."

Tomas swore. "That's going to take a while, and Finn will have to get it cleared."

Marie turned to spot me walking down the incline. "They had to get word somehow."

"I'll get it started, Pyre." Finn sounded more confident of the process than Tomas had. "When do you want a flight prepped?"

"Now. I'll be staying the night here. There are two groups coming in that require my attendance. I'll coordinate what I can from here, and you'll pick up the slack, Finn."

"Got it, Pyre."

I stopped a dozen paces from her. There were likely quite a few Consociation officials concerned about Clara's situation. It made sense that they would want information, but Marie's time would be better spent finding the witch, if she were that important.

Those above Finn and Marie might also be concerned about the shakeup of our team; we'd rid ourselves of Stacey and all the difficulty she'd caused, and now we had a breach at the office. We might not appear like we were functioning at optimum.

As we drew closer, Marie turned from her study of

David and the submerged SUV and gestured to our vests. "Do I need to hold you for healing?"

"I'm fine," Leah said.

I pressed against my tender stomach, but after I'd already done two or three quick healings with the Earth realm, I didn't think it was serious. "I'm okay. We can't assume Lambert will be heading to Daytona."

"What do you have, Kristen?"

"Nothing. That's the problem."

"I'll not have you sit here and wait on Finn and Tomas. The locals' search will yield something in time for you to focus on that, or you'll be in the air. Even if they don't take Clara and Bea to Daytona, you can dig into Lambert's connections, and that might get us a lead."

She was right. A clue in Daytona might give us what we needed to track them down before anything bad happened to Bea and Clara. I grimaced, remembering Phillip's corpse. "Understood. Finn, do we have any leads of where to look?"

"Two addresses. I'm still digging."

TWELVE

While the local FBI gave David, Leah, and me a ride back to the Demopolis airport, we decided that we'd need a quick change of clothes before we stunk up the plane. Leah and I both had clothes in our go bags we could switch into, but David's were soaked in pond water and smelled worse than we did.

"There's got to be a clothing store in town." David sat in front with a somber woman in her mid-fifties who'd shown zero interest in his charm.

"Not in Livingston, that I know of."

"A laundromat," David gestured to a brick building off to our right. It was dark inside the windows and no cars parked in front.

"David, I'll have clothes waiting for you in Daytona." Finn used his more diplomatic tone, though I could tell he was stressed after a very long, intense day.

The woman sighed. "Most people just hit Walmart up in Demopolis. It's about fifteen minutes up the road from the airport."

"Walmart. Okay. I can't be choosy."

"No, David. I'm not holding the flight an extra half an hour to an hour for you to go shopping. Daytona." Finn was firm over the comms.

David sighed. "No Walmart. Too far away."

We were driving up the main road of Livingston, and most businesses other than churches and gas stations appeared closed.

"Dollar General," our driver offered.

"Definitely," Leah said.

We shifted over and took a left turn, with David turning back to glare at us. "Snacks," I said.

It took me no time to check out with cheese sticks for dinner, some iced tea, and an ice cream sandwich while David whined in another aisle. We were back in the FBI's SUV when he finally walked out with a very small bag.

"What did you find?" Leah asked, almost gleefully. He tossed the bag back to her. "Ooh, a three-pack of tagless tanks. White. Are those gym shorts?"

We changed on board the plane, and I pressed more of Earth realm's mud-like healing over my bruised stomach. Leah took no time to come out in a rose-colored skirt and top that looked ironed.

David came out of the tiny bathroom to Leah videoing the new wardrobe for Finn and Tomas. "The girls are going to love the shorts, David."

He dropped into his chair with a glower and buckled himself in. "I'm hoping you have better options for me in Daytona, Finn."

"I'm working on it. What I'm not having luck is finding the coven leader's residence who was working with Lambert. They're known to use a hunting camp west of the city, but I had two associates and the local police confirm the site is empty. The three others known to be connected have left town, and their apartments are empty."

"They might have been part of the crew that attacked us," said Leah.

"Likely. I'm getting local warrants for searches, just to keep it all clean. I'd like to find someone we can talk to, though."

The plane taxied quickly, and I plucked out my phone before takeoff. "Let me check with my friend, Yaz. She might be able to dig something up before we land."

"Thanks. Otherwise, I have a list of properties to search. It's going to be late, after eight, when you land. I've had local enforcement locate most of their vehicles. Their phones haven't been on in a few days. They've just disappeared, so I think we know who we just tangled with. Maybe their apartments will give us a place to look next. I'll send you a list of names we know of."

An hour later, I was forwarding Finn and Tomas an address off Tomaka Farms Road in Port Orange, just south of Daytona Beach. My comms were charged well over halfway, so I put them back in and tapped them on. "Finn. Did you get it?"

"Yeah. Running the address now."

"This Oscar Rainer has been a lone witch for three decades. He has strong anti-Consociation opinions that help keep him isolated. Over the past three weeks, he's made a stir trying to recruit members of covens to a resistance that will overcome the authority of the Consociation. There has been no public interest in his offers, but he is the loudest Yaz has heard of in a while. She's not heard of Lambert, but the leaders of that coven are Genevieve and Scott, and it's a larger coven than just four. Give her time, and she'll have some more names."

Tomas hadn't said much through the day, and I expected him to have some comment about the extra searches. He remained quiet. I considered texting Finn, but left it alone. I wanted to know if they'd run phones from the airports. If I were being honest, it was to see if Bea had betrayed us rather than prove her innocence. Guilt tugged at my face.

I waited a couple of minutes before Finn responded about Oscar Rainer. "We've got a similar profile on him, but we don't have any update on his recruitment. We'll have more information about any potential connection to Lambert or the coven soon."

"A lot of data to cover," I said before realizing I was fishing. "Thanks."

We hadn't heard from Marie since we left, and our plans for Daytona weren't firm. I had questions about Bea, and even Clara. This case was a mess.

"What's got you worried?" asked David.

I tried to flash a happy smile. "All of it?"

Leah looked up from her phone to answer. "How'd they find us, and where'd they go? Bothers me too, but we've all been mulling it over. I think we're on the best course. You got us another lead. It's late. I'll be up for a nap soon. If one of us had a better idea, we'd be doing it."

Tomas spoke up sharply. "Bigger problems. Finn's on with Daytona Beach's District 1 Captain. One of the patrols got too close to a car on our APB list. The window exploded, injuring an officer. She's at the hospital, and the unit is in an uproar. They've got the area cordoned off and consider it an active bomb threat."

David laughed. "I really hope I don't have to show up at that party in these clothes."

"How bad was the officer hurt?" I asked.

Tomas took a second. "Lacerations. Finn will have

local FBI waiting for you when you land. The rain has stopped."

"They'll be waiting with some clothes, right? Tomas?" No one answered David.

CHAPTER

THIRTEEN

A taco in my hand, I slid out of my seatbelt in the back of the Chevy Suburban to a sea of blue and red lights clogging a damp cul-de-sac. Clouds gave a dark background to the well-kept suburban neighborhood.

"Is this the rave?" David wore a gray turtleneck and black slacks, obviously more comfortable since he'd ditched the gym shorts in a garbage bin. When we'd arrived at a posh private jet terminal in Daytona Beach, he gathered most of the attention with his outfit. Dollar General hadn't meshed with a holstered weapon at his side and badge clipped to his belt.

"Feds." The officer who let us through the barricades frowned at David's attempted humor and called through on her radio.

Still sticky with sweat, I hadn't opted for Kevlar under my second suit of the day. The night smelled fresh after the showers we'd missed while in Alabama.

Leah had driven and paused behind the wheel. "You take the lead, David."

What appeared to be two different departments were bearing down on him with each officer snapping glances at the other. David whispered over the comms. "Kristen, see what we have going on over there."

I took a crispy bite of my second taco, careful not to drip sour cream, and strode toward the cordoned vehicle. The passenger window was gone, and a man walked a dog a good six feet from the car. An older Camaro, black with red pins, stood under heavy spotlights.

David attempted to placate the locals, a district captain and someone from another department.

Finn grumbled at the interaction. "FBI is twenty minutes out, and I can only get two of them with a tow truck."

I began tugging at Dur-Alf, searching for wards, then after the day's activities, searched Mer and Haven as well. Nothing flared up, but I almost tripped and dropped my taco when one of the nearby officers stiffened and locked his attention on me. A witch was rare but not unusual in law enforcement. I'd been a witch and lead detective before I transferred to the DRC.

We couldn't be too careful in this situation. Diverting to the side of the Camaro, I didn't give the man any notice, though he was following my movements through the officers and vehicles. "Leah, can you get a picture of someone for me? Get it to Finn or Tomas for identification? My tugs on the realms caught an officer's interest. It could be an innocent witch on the force, or we've got someone connected to the coven showing some interest."

"Got it. Point me in the right direction." I could see her break off from David's back and scan the surrounding crowd.

"Back end of the Camaro. White male, thirties, five-eleven, athletic. Alone behind a pair of older officers joking about something."

"I see your stalker. You just looking for a date?" she asked.

"Definitely not."

"Finn, Tomas. You'll have to brighten them up a bit."

I waited, but no biting remark from Tomas. Frowning, I stood facing the passenger side of the Camaro with our witch to my left side. He hadn't made a move to leave. I hoped that my nibbling on the taco appeared nonchalant enough.

"Manny Fournier. He and his wife are members of a separate coven than Lambert's, but there are connections. I'm sending her picture to your phones along with addresses, vehicles, and children's info. Finn, can you get me access to their phones and dig into their coven?"

"Give me a minute. Team, don't approach Manny at this moment. Maybe we can use him to lead us somewhere we don't have on the map."

I finished my taco and wadded up the wrapper. "Well, I don't see any more wards; do we want to search the vehicle? Manny's focused on me, so maybe pull back, Leah, to keep an eye on him while David makes a show of it."

"Let's do this!" David started for the Camaro, causing the local enforcement to get skittish and jump in to stop him.

"Wait for me to clear it, David." Finn's temper tinged his tone. We all needed a break, but Lambert had Clara and Bea, and we couldn't rest. They needed us.

Kneading the ball of trash in my right hand, I carefully focused on David, leaving Manny to Leah. It took a moment for Finn's requests to filter through the group, but after two minutes they had the officer and dog removed to a safe distance.

"Have at it," said one of the older officers. The unspoken, "blow yourselves up if you want to," was evident in his tone and gesture.

The vehicle belonged to Steward "Stew" Samson. He'd been part of the coven associated with Lambert since the 1990s. Other than a strong passion for Wiccan symbolism, Led Zeppelin, lavender, and sage, his Camaro was in show-ready quality with only tools in the trunk.

"I've got nothing to indicate another site," I said over the comms.

"Me neither." David flicked a piece of glass off his slacks. "What's the call, boss — Oscar's place like we planned, or stalk this Manny fellow?"

"Manny," answered Finn. "We got a clean go-ahead on his phone and his wife's. They've been texting up a storm while he's been here. Make a show of taking off, then find somewhere to sit dark for a moment. We can get you back behind him if he keeps his phone on."

"Oscar's cell isn't on," Tomas added.

"I'll warm up the car," said Leah. "I can watch better from the street if he tries to race us out of here."

David stepped to the circle of officers and nodded to the older man. "All clear. FBI should be here with a tow truck." He grinned pointedly at one of the younger female officers. "We'll be here all night if you want to get with us."

I groaned and spun pointedly to march for Leah, weaving through the patrol cars. Manny had faded farther to the side, avoiding us and the officers.

Ignoring Iliodor's possible part in this, Lambert had certainly been involved with Phillip's death and Tomas's attack, along with the abduction of Clara and Bea. Despite aliases, some of the Daytona witches had been identified from the jet in Alabama.

We still didn't know how they tracked us, though it was

a moot point presently. If Bea were involved, we would have bigger issues, as would other parts of the Consociation. Oscar and Manny's involvement might prove more relevant for rescuing Clara.

David jogged up beside me. "Probably should grab that Kevlar."

"Agreed," said Finn over the comms.

The night was starting to cool, but I didn't relish the idea. Despite numerous healings, I felt the bruises. Leah heard us over the comms and passed the front to open up the back where our gear was stored.

Manny made no move to leave his secluded post. I jabbed a finger past the barricades. "What does Manny drive, Finn?"

"I sent the reports," snapped Tomas, "but, tacos, right?"

Heat flushed up my face. We were going to have a chat.

"Black Camry," answered Finn.

"Parked three houses down outside the barricade."

Masking our activities, Leah and I slid on Kevlar vests and adjusted holsters. David rattled mints from his passenger seat.

"When you leave, take the first right. There's a church you can circle and park behind to keep out of sight."

"Got it." Leah shifted us into gear and turned up the air conditioning.

As we backed up and turned toward the barricades, Manny moved up the sidewalk at a brisk pace. I kept him in sight while Leah paused for the officer to give us a frown before letting us out.

I grabbed three waters out of the back. "He's leaving." He might have easily hung around to see what happened to the car.

We drove leisurely down the street, so I twisted about

to watch. I'd been correct about his car. I would review all the reports once we had a moment, thankful I had caught up somewhat on the flight.

His lights were on, and he backed up quickly as we neared the corner. When we turned, he sped to keep up.

"Well, this is awkward," I said. "*He's* following *us*." There was also concern he might be prepping us for an attack, but I'd see where this went.

Finn's tone pitched in surprise and his faint southern drawl emerged. "Damn. Alright. Change in plans. Turn right down the dead end across from the church."

David twisted around to see past me. "What's his plan? Find out if we know anything?"

"His wife has been on a couple of sites. I'll track them and see if we have a message drop." My lips twisted at Tomas's interested tone.

Leah pulled onto a road with four duplexes. The police lights from the cul-de-sac flashed behind the two on our left. "Where's he going?"

I groaned. "He shut his lights off and is parking in the church parking lot."

David chuckled. He never seemed tired, and Leah had taken two power naps on the flight. I was dragging. Leah parked where we could see him, but left our lights on and engine running.

"I'll clear him off your tail." Finn's tone had returned to its tired droning. "Give me a minute."

It took nearly ten minutes before a squad car pulled into the church parking lot on the opposite end. I flinched. "Finn — Manny's wearing a false uniform. They'll take him in."

"We *know* about his uniform," Tomas said in his best condescending tone.

"My instructions to the police were to park there and

not investigate anything until I released them. Considering the ruckus nearby, they didn't appreciate the request."

Manny's car started up and left the parking lot.

"Brilliant, Finn." David sounded appreciative. It *had* been a good move.

I relaxed in my seat and doubted Manny would lead us anywhere constructive. He'd been focused on us.

We spent the next fifteen minutes doing a large lap through the neighborhood where he couldn't find us, because we were a good distance behind him, then followed him to his house. Leah idled the Suburban along the side of the road, a couple hundred feet from his driveway.

"Oscar Rainer's?" I asked. We had intended to do a quiet check on his house without making ourselves known. It was almost 10 p.m., and he might be asleep. That might make the task easier, but less conclusive.

Finn responded over the comms. "Kristen, try to get close enough to detect any life signs. I bet they got Clara and Bea in transport, but I'll take any lead at this point." His tone made me wonder if he considered them already lost to us.

My chest remained tight as Leah drove us in the dark to Oscar's. I worried that they would torture them, and also about my concerns over Bea. I didn't want to believe she would betray us, but couldn't drop the nagging thought.

Oscar's house was dark, and I would have considered abandoned from the fallen gate and the high brush growing around the building. We passed slowly, then Leah pulled off the unlit back highway after the next locked gate.

"You're in the lead, Kristen," she said as she turned off the engine.

I hopped out with distant car lights driving toward us. "Well, I won't have to hop a fence." Instinctively, I tugged at the realms, searching for wards. "Wait out here in case I come running out."

The air had cooled enough not to sweat immediately, but I was nervous, and that wouldn't help. Before I reached the broken gate, the oncoming car passed without slowing. I kept testing for wards. I risked a Haven detection spell into the yard. If a witch was awake inside and close to the front, they'd see the white traces around me as well as themselves. The woods were heavy with small creatures, but nothing large enough to cause concern.

"Here goes." I stepped carefully between the metal bars of the fence, wincing as my boots crunched on debris. Luckily it had rained, softening the worst.

If someone did live here, they wanted it to appear abandoned. Weeds grew high, and dark windows had dead vines across them. I kept at the search for wards and tossed Haven across the front door.

Ghostly shapes formed in my vision behind the house as cats or possums scurried away. There was no one inside except a nest of something small such as rats or mice.

I leaned close to the window, gaining cobwebs in my hair but no hint of what was inside. Risking a little light, I turned my phone flashlight on and pointed it in. There was furniture and pictures on the wall. "Someone lives here, or used to," I whispered into the comms. "Empty at the moment. I'm going to walk around it."

Keeping the flashlight on, I traipsed through high weeds and bumped against a tire and rim that grass had grown through. Behind the house, I checked wards and threw Haven, only to light up more critters and birds. A path of worn grass led to the driveway and another gate.

"I'm going farther back." To the right, leading deeper

into the woods, a gate was locked with a no trespassing sign. "Is there a different property in the back, or is it part of his lot?"

"Yes — properties are separate. No connections between owners that we could find."

I turned left and shut off my phone as I headed down the drive. "No one here. No leads."

Leah answered, "I hear you behind us. Meet you at the other gate."

"Yeah." I was tired and disappointed. We'd found nothing that would lead to Clara. Manny was someone new, but unless Tomas dug up something, it didn't help us.

The gate creaked ahead of me, and I made out David and Leah in the darkness. None of us spoke as we headed for the Suburban.

"Kristen's suggestion got us some answers," Finn said over the comms.

FOURTEEN

"Nothing useful," Tomas added.

"We'll see," answered Finn. "We've got a lead that the FBI in Atlanta will track down. We think we can find out who alerted Iliodor's people about our destination. A burner phone was communicating from DeKalb to another at the Fulton air strip. They're both off now, but we'll pull video."

"When?" I wanted Bea to be innocent.

"Just before we arrived. Probably just after they filed the flight plan."

I smiled. "That's good."

"Why?" asked Finn.

My cheeks flushed, but I said it anyway. "No one we know, then."

Leah glanced at me before she opened the driver's door. Her quizzical expression faded and she nodded, shrugging with a tilt of her head. "Have to consider everything."

"What?" asked David.

"Bea," Finn answered. "We'd already cleared her communications."

I could have saved myself some guilt if I'd just asked. "So, what's the plan, boss?" We all need some rest.

"Grab a couple of hours shut-eye. If they drove there, they won't arrive until 3 a.m., maybe. Tomas, do you have the team at the same hotel?"

"Yes." No biting remark for Finn.

If I'd asked, I'd have gotten something snarky. "Do we have a plan for 3 a.m.?"

"I'm hoping we'll have something for you to work on by then."

"No sleep?"

"Did a twenty-minute power nap while you were flying. I'm good." He didn't sound like it.

Leah did a three-point turn and headed toward Daytona Beach. I leaned back in the seat and closed my eyes. Now I could worry about them torturing Bea as well as Clara. I was glad Finn had considered the same possibility; it eased the guilt a little.

"Mind if I take a cruise down to some of the bars? It's still early." I couldn't be sure who David asked.

Finn answered. "Don't. I might be calling with something you need to jump on."

"I wouldn't promise David that." I was tired.

David chuckled. "Risqué."

My phone vibrated in my pocket, and I slid it out.

"Call?" Jade texted.

"How long before we get to the hotel?" I asked.

David waved his screen at me. "Twenty-five."

"Thirty minutes? I'm driving with everyone."

"Okay."

"I'll call then, Honey."

Jade hadn't been big on calling lately, so I straightened in my seat, wondering what she might need to talk about. We still had a visit to plan for the summer; I wasn't going to miss it.

The hotel smelled like Pine-Sol when we arrived. We took the elevator together.

David shook the clothes bag on his shoulder. "Might need to get something to wear if we're here another day."

I had enough clothes, but I needed a shower. "I don't think Clara and Bea have that much time."

Leah nodded, frowning.

My room was down an outside walkway on the second floor. I stripped my jacket off, pulled out my comms, and dropped my bag on the bed as I crossed to the back balcony where I could see the beach. Waves crashed in a low rumble.

I sat and pressed Jade's number. "Hi, Honey."

"Hey, Mom."

"Everything okay? Is this about the trip this summer? I promise I'll make it happen if I have shoot myself in the foot to get leave."

"I had a vision." Her voice trembled. She hated them.

Cold poured over me, and I tensed. "What was it?"

"Don't know. Not Tarus, and I don't think you were part of it." Her voice lifted at the last part.

I silently took a deep breath. "Tell me about it."

"There was a cave. Wet rocks. Something big was there. Hairy."

I swallowed. There was nothing I could do to protect her from these. They were rare. "Werewolf?"

"I don't know. I never saw the face. It was eating something and hunched over. I just knew it was big."

"Well, was anyone you know there?" Knowing something about someone you cared about was the worst.

"Not that I know of. Maybe it was me." Her tone tightened. "I'm scared."

"Okay. That's normal. We know that." It sounded like a werewolf. "If it is a werewolf, they are just people with a condition. Same emotions. Same kindness." I couldn't tell her about Leah.

"I guess. It was still scary."

I stared out at the waves and got the conversation to different topics until we were chuckling about my mishaps with camping. Promising not to embarrass her too much in front of her friends, she seemed in a better mood when we were done talking.

It was late by the time I turned on the shower and stripped in earnest. I needed to sleep, but washing off some of the day was a requirement. Clara and Bea wouldn't have the luxury.

We still hadn't heard from Marie. Our hopes rested on Tomas and Finn tracking down a lead for us. For all I knew, we'd be flying out in the morning.

I stepped under the hot water and let the spray pour over me.

FIFTEEN

I woke in the dark, unsure whether someone had knocked. Sitting up, my skin prickled as if someone were watching me. The scent of the ocean wafted through the open balcony doors with the gentle roll of waves on the beach.

My cell had charged beside the bed. I opened it, but hadn't received any texts, just emails from Tomas and Finn. It was just after midnight; I should be sleeping.

Uneasy, I reached into Haven to toss a ward into my room and blushed. I'd used it as a teen when the creeps would tell me something or someone was under my bed or in the empty house.

My breath caught as I noticed Haven already lit a person who slept in the next room. Someone else had thrown a detection spell. A ghostly shape moved outside my door. They crouched and appeared to be gesturing furiously — as if setting a ward. I jumped up, and they reacted, seeing my movement in Haven.

A dim trail of Dur-Alf followed my stalker as they jumped off the second floor walkway in front of my room.

I took two steps in my long night shirt, then stopped. If they'd finished a ward, I could be blasting the door and myself. Even with a shield, I'd set the whole hotel in turmoil, and I wouldn't want to go chasing the witch without equipment and backup.

My comms had charged green, and I dropped it into my ear. "Tomas, Finn, I've got an issue." I might have been the last door they painted with a ward. "*We've* got an issue."

Finn coughed. His voice was shaken as if awakened. "What?"

"Someone used Haven on my room and was attempting to or has placed a ward on my door. They spooked when I got up."

"Don't — okay, what's your plan?"

"Contact Leah and David. Have them hold tight. I'm going to try and check it from my side." I faced the door and tugged on Dur-Alf to light up the interlocking sigils. "It's a blast spell."

"Let me get them. How thick is the door?" I could hear him typing in the background.

"Thin enough to try." I knelt at the door, careful not to touch it. A ward embedded itself on the surface, but had depth. This one overlapped the frame to activate on opening or touch from the other side.

Finn's voice muffled as he spoke with Leah over his phone. I hadn't paid attention to their room numbers, but they were on the same floor.

I pulled up a shield from Dur-Alf and covered my body as well as possible, leaving a hole to reach through. A half inch from the surface of the door, I tugged at the realm and pulled toward me, pinching and wrapping Dur-Alf like taffy. My eye ticked as the ward shifted, puckering through.

Digging in a finger, I frayed the binding with my fingertip. Wisps of dust floated to the floor, then the entire ward popped.

I let out a long sigh.

"You got it," Finn said. I hadn't even realized he'd been waiting for me to react.

"Let me get dressed. What are their room numbers?"

"Tomas, text their room numbers to Kristen. I've got a message in to local FBI. I want someone watching the building until we get you out of there. We'll need you to check the vehicle as well."

My hands trembled slightly as I pulled off my shirt and unhooked my hangers from the shower rod. "How'd they find us, Finn?"

"Don't know." He cleared his throat. "Since you're up; Pyre's on her way to Daytona."

My hair was a fright, but I didn't have time to worry about it. "Not on comms?" Obviously. I cringed, waiting for Tomas to say something. "When does she get here?"

"Forty minutes to the airport. I had local FBI driving her over, but I think now I'll get a fresh vehicle."

I strode to my bed and shoved on shoes. "Does she have a room?"

"Yes. Tomas, make sure to send her that number as well."

"Already did." His tone was sharp, but not as snark as if I'd asked.

Was I just being too sensitive? "Thanks."

I kept a shield up when I opened my door with gun in hand. The street was quiet, though I could hear cars. The parking lot was well lit, and no one fired at me or tossed a spell in my direction.

Tugging at the realms, I made my way to the first door,

David's. The same ward covered his. "They tagged David."

"I wouldn't want to be left out; that would be insulting." I could hear him plainly through the comms, but he was just inside as well.

"Back up, David." It only took a second to pluck holes in the ward. Without commenting when I finished, I continued to Marie's room. "Nothing on Marie's door." That might give us a hint how they tracked us down.

Leah's was warded as well, and David popped his door as I was working on the ward. He mimed an explosion when I glanced at him. "Leah's clear. Vehicle?"

"Take David, if he's dressed."

He plucked at his suit lapel, then crooked his head forward, studying me. Still silent, he motioned around his head as if it were lopsided. I didn't appreciate his appraisal of my hair and glowered appropriately.

Leah opened the door wearing a cherry-blossom pink outfit and a holstered weapon. She'd done her makeup. "I'll go too. So, Pyre's coming here to whip us into shape?"

Our comms crackled. "I'm here to help. What the hell is going on over there? I got Finn's message." As Marie spoke, Leah raised her eyebrows, but hardly seemed upset.

I tapped at my curls and grimaced at how off they were. "A witch warded our doors with blasting spells." David headed for the elevator, and I followed with Leah.

"I got that much."

Awkwardly, I shoved my weapon into my waistband behind my back. "We're checking the car. Everyone's clear. They didn't hit your room."

"Considerate of them. Any details on who it was?"

There weren't any cameras in the hall. "I'd guess they were male from their build, but I barely got a glimpse through Haven. Average height for a man. Jumped off the walkway onto the parking lot. I'd guess he used a Dur-Alf shield to cut the distance short."

"David, check the front desk."

"Sounds like a plan, Pyre. Any news from high above?"

She *had* spent a long time out of communication. I'd expected her to brief someone and come right back to us. It had been short of half a day since we'd heard from her.

"No. They've sent us some resources from out west. They'll be here late morning."

"Resources? Not *Mika*." David rolled his eyes at me.

"Get over it." Marie shut him down as if she'd expected his comment.

I'd never heard the name, but I wasn't going to ask with the comms live.

David huffed good-naturedly when we stepped out of the elevator and approached the abandoned counter. "Hello."

Flicking a shield ahead of us, I let Leah lead the way out the front doors. Lights lit the parking lot and road. Salt air ruffled my hair, but no one attacked us.

We'd parked by the wall to the left. I tugged at the realms while scanning the streets. There were no pedestrians this early on a Tuesday morning, and the only car was a lone truck ambling toward the north.

While I searched for wards, David politely grilled the late night counter person until we were all pretty sure the employee had been asleep. He did have access to the video, and David worked with the man to review it.

"I'm not picking up anything." I'd searched everywhere on our Suburban and didn't find a ward.

Leah stood attentively in the parking lot, watching the neighboring buildings and street. I joined her, but let my shield drop with a shrug. The church we'd visited on Sunday and the woods we'd searched were across the road.

Lambert had been willing to kill, or have killed, one of the clergy just to goad us into leaving the office. He'd tortured Phillip to death and used his illusion to hurt Tomas. What could we expect with Bea and Clara? Time was running out to find them before he did something nasty. Iliodor might be involved, or not, but I worried about Lambert's actions more.

"Pyre, are we on the road when you get here?" Leah led the way back to the hotel.

"Yes, we'll follow up on Finn's location immediately."

I glanced at Leah in surprise before asking, "Where's that, Finn?"

He sighed over the comms. "It might be nothing. We had three hits from coven members' phones connected to Lambert on a location west of the city. Other than known residences, it is the only convergence over the past thirty days."

Leah's eyes flashed wide, and she shoved me toward the door. As I stumbled and lost my balance, gunshots popped in the night. Hands scraping on the ground, I toppled as a Dur-Alf crushing spell clipped my left shoulder before it smashed glass into the lobby. Aluminum frames groaned.

"Two by the road." Leah had been spun from the edge of the spell and stopped in a crouch for the barest second. Her weapon was out, and she fired once as she darted sideways.

I threw a shield behind me, ground my knees into a rising turn, and dug for my weapon at my back. I'd assumed the attacker had left, but he'd waited for another chance.

A man tugged into Dur-Alf with a flicker of the realm at his left side. Leah flashed along the cars parked at the front, about to be clear for a shot.

I stood, exposed at the front of the building with no quick cover. He'd timed his ambush well.

"Watch out." Digging out a shield, I tossed it at the same time he threw a new crushing spell into her path. The Dur-Alf spells ground in puffs of moss-green dust, but glass still shattered from the sedan parked there.

Leah caught some of the shrapnel and fired a shot heedless of the clashing magic.

A second man, better hidden at the edge of the next property to the north, tried to slide a binding spell onto me by curving around my shield. Even holding two spells, I adjusted in time to stop it and fired my weapon at the first man who targeted Leah. He jerked but didn't go down.

David darted out of the hotel, crunching in the glass.

My more distant shield had stopped Leah from being crushed but interfered with her gunfire. Both attackers pulled up shields, and the one farther away threw a binding spell.

Picking up speed on his second stride, David catapulted in the air as the binding caught him.

The man I'd hit was drawing back, but Leah darted between parked cars and into the street out of my sight. She hit him with a headshot and began emptying her weapon at the second man.

I could see his shield flicking puffs of Dur-Alf as I jogged toward David. When the attacker's shield bobbed to the side, I hit him with a solid binding spell and smiled smugly as it wrapped him tight.

One of the difficulties in working as the lone witch is that no one can see your spells. Leah's last shot hit him in the neck. She didn't know he couldn't move until he toppled stiff.

I winced as she swore. "Crap." Her tone said she regretted it. None of the team were prone to killing.

I tossed Haven at the neighboring property, but I could see a sedan with running lights parked down the road. Just in case, I threw a shield in front of Leah and kept it in pace with her as she approached the dying men. Their bodies were fading ghosts in the detection spell.

"Sorry. I should have said something." Neither of us would have had the time to react to that situation. I leaned down and dug the binding spell off David. "Two attackers down," I said for the benefit of Finn and Marie.

"I hate binding spells." David jumped up and inspected his scuffed suit. His cheek had a red scrape on it that he found with his hand soon enough. Turning toward the hotel, he brushed at his clothes.

"Anybody hurt?" Marie asked.

"David's wardrobe. I'm okay. Leah?" I was approaching her, still holding the shield, as she reached the first body.

"Scratches. I'm fine." Despite her being a werewolf, I rarely heard her angry, but her tone growled in frustration.

Sirens sounded in the distance. "Finn, we're going to need a call to local enforcement."

He brought his phone closer, and I could hear it ringing. As someone answered, Finn turned off his comms mike.

I reached the man I'd helped kill as Leah moved to check the other, and I belatedly released the binding. The shields I left up, though Haven showed nothing more than a cat walking in the nearby parking lot.

Killing someone always tore at me a little. Standing on the quiet street with the scent of gunpowder, it had time to sink in as I stared at his face. Marie wasn't saying anything, and the only muted voice on the comms was David talking with the slightly hysterical employee.

From the reports, I knew all the witches in Daytona

that we suspected might be working with Lambert, and this wasn't one. It wasn't Manny. There were covens here than we knew of. Gun in hand, I pulled out my phone and sent a picture of the corpse to Tomas.

The sirens grew close, and I turned to find the lights of two cars racing down the empty street. I'd left my badge upstairs. Hopefully, Finn would get it cleared up before they pulled weapons on us.

David spoke loudly over the comms. "Sending you some footage of our little visitor, Tomas. He's got his nose and mouth covered, but you're magic with this kind of stuff."

Tomas swore in annoyance. We did expect a lot from him.

The video likely would match one of the men dead on the street in front of me.

SIXTEEN

When Marie arrived, I was packing my go bag in my room while David entertained the police on the street. Finn had done his best, but the suspicious locals were cranky and demanding, even after one of their captains made it to the scene.

"David, move it. Get packed. Everyone downstairs." Marie's comms picked up the surrounding chatter before she cut them to deal with an officer who was trying to argue with her before she was able to introduce herself. I knew it wouldn't go well for him.

Our two dead witches were out of Texas and attached to a roving coven known to work with Iliodor. I had little room left to suggest that he wasn't involved. Tomas had matched one of the corpses with the video of our visitor who'd slipped into the lobby earlier in the night.

"On my way down," I said into my comms, unsure who was on at the moment. The air was cool, low in the seventies, but I was sweating from our skirmish downstairs. Purse and backpack over my shoulder, I wore a suit jacket over my holster and planned to add a Kevlar vest once I got downstairs. At least I'd remembered to clip my flashlight on my belt.

I started when I stepped out of my room. Three guests were leaning on the railing, watching the police, or had been until I shuffled out. "What's going on?" a woman in a nightshirt asked me.

I offered an apologetic smile and headed inside the main hotel without an answer. The lobby held more guests up, milling about, and trading theories. I darted past the counter and crunched through glass toward Leah standing in the parking lot with her light bag. "I'm ready to get out of here," I said quietly as I leaned toward her.

Marie squared off against three officers at the north entrance to the parking lot, where the bodies were being trundled off by emergency vehicles. Police cars blocked all lanes of traffic and barricaded the sidewalks. Ours wasn't the only hotel awakened by the gunfire.

Leah nodded toward two SUVs parked in the road to the south. "Local FBI, but they haven't gotten out of their vehicles yet. No one's happy with this whole mess."

Flashing police lights flooded the night street that crawled with over a dozen officers. The two FBI vehicles were dark and still against the activity. They were supposed to take over for us during these scenarios. "Finn?"

"Yeah." His tone was distracted.

"What's up with the local FBI?"

"Evidently, I'm waiting for someone to wake up. The rest of the department keeps deferring any decision until they get a response. It won't affect you." His slightly southern accent deepened, and frustration tinged his comments.

Adjusting my bag and purse, I pulled out my phone

and checked the team's email for the reports. I wasn't sure where we were going, except someplace west.

The address was to a house with a barn off West International Speedway Boulevard out of Daytona Beach. Besides the forest, the only property nearby belonged to the state. A dirt road ran behind both of those. "There are two entrances." I showed the map to Leah. "If they've brought Clara and Bea there, they'll ward the entries."

David sauntered out of the broken hotel, noting us, then Marie. "What's the plan?" he asked Leah. The knees of his suit were scuffed; that had to bother him.

She gestured toward my cell. "We were going over the location now. Finn, did Marie have a plan?"

"Adjacent property, scan from west fence, then approach."

The state grounds appeared to be sheds and equipment. It was probably gated, but we could clear that. Dirt roads led around the water between the two properties. There were a couple of trees on the border, but not much cover.

Leah flicked a finger, alerting me to Marie's approach. The men she'd been talking to were clustered, and her grimace said she wasn't pleased. Tapping her comms on, she began speaking with Finn, "Wrangle them as you can, Finn. I'm leaving. Tomas, do we have anything on small flights into any of the local Daytona airstrips or out of Alabama or Mississippi near Clara's?"

"Nothing, Pyre. If they are coming to Daytona, they didn't take a flight. Everything out of that part of Alabama and locale I've cleared. They're on the road."

"If they are coming to Daytona, they'd have arrived by now, Pyre." Finn's tone hinted that Daytona was a long shot, and he was right.

We had a small chance that Lambert would head to

home ground, but we'd also been spotted here. He might already be taking Bea and Clara elsewhere.

Marie strode past, leading us toward the Suburban. "Grab our gear. I've got a car parked on the street." As we dug out our vests and supplies we'd left in the SUV, she grabbed armfuls and marched for the wash of flashing police lights. "Tomas is tracking any hint of a connection. Until we have another direction to follow, we're jumping on anything in Daytona that came on our radar. First is the Speedway Boulevard farm."

"Slim chance is better than none?" asked David.

"Exactly." She passed the two FBI vehicles and led us to a tan Pontiac G6 with a scrape down the left side. David gestured to the dent in the passenger door, and she cut him off. "Came that way." Juggling equipment, she opened the small trunk. "Shove it in there. I've got a feeling Lambert is heading back here, especially since they focused on stopping you. Why bother if they're headed to Albuquerque or Canada?"

David grabbed a vest. "Mika?"

"Get over it." Marie slid on hers. "A unit lead like me, Kristen."

I hadn't even glanced at her, but she knew I was out of the loop on this. "ETA, Tomas?"

"Landing 10:11 a.m. Eastern, Pyre."

She grimaced and wiped a hand over her bald scalp. "It's after 3 a.m. now, so over six hours. I'd love them on this. We can't wait. David, you got the address?"

He nodded, pulling out his phone. "Yep, half an hour, Pyre." He folded into the front seat as I closed the trunk.

Marie had the engine revving by the time I closed the door and scrambled for my seatbelt. Tires chirped when she spun about and headed south. The police diverting traffic gave us sharp glances.

From our earlier discussions, Lambert could just be arriving in Daytona, if they drove here. "We're coming in through the west side of the property, except for Leah. I'm dropping you off just short of the entry from the main road, and you'll come in from the southeast."

"Got it, Pyre." Leah leaned back casually, watching the quiet streets we passed.

"Kristen, no Haven. If anyone is there, they won't be asleep, and they're all witches, so you'll announce us if you do. We'll be looking for vehicles and movement to indicate someone's there. Check for wards, but don't light up the realms for them. David, Leah, we'll be using our senses."

My lip twitched. "Well, Oscar's missing, and Manny and his wife were a surprise addition; so were the people from Texas. Let's assume we have six left from the initial attack. How many do you expect there, if everyone has arrived from Alabama?" We might have a dozen, or more.

"Tomas, any luck on that trace on the Texans?"

"Not yet, Pyre. Those two flew in on different flights, but both out of Houston. Exactly as Iliodor would have planned it. I'm checking each known associate who booked a flight. Nothing so far, but he's been known to use rail and car. He could be drawing off multiple covens as well."

"Night storms. I hate being so far behind his moves."

The roads were quiet, especially as we drove farther west. Marie raced down the stretches between traffic lights. After one, there were no more streetlights on the split highway, and pines lined the right side with the hint of a canal or a deep ditch with reeds growing in it.

A truck passed us from the other direction, but otherwise it seemed we were alone on the highway. "Two minutes to the property, Pyre." David waggled his phone.

Leah leaned forward between the front seats. "You're going to slow down when you drop me off, right?"

Marie scoffed. "You ready?"

Pulling an FBI windbreaker up from the floor, Leah flipped it inside out and slipped it over her Kevlar vest and bright sleeves. Her pants were still colorful, but from the height of the brush on the roadside, I doubted anyone would see her.

We began slowing down, and I definitely saw water between the grass and the forest. The pines had thinned out, letting some oak and elm crop up along with palmetto palms.

"Good luck," I said as we rumbled to a stop off the divided highway.

"Thanks." Leah slipped out to the marshy scent of water with hints of pine and earthy spring growth. I didn't relish her trek through the brush.

We rolled back onto the highway, and Marie passed a dark property where I only caught a glimpse of roof trim braced with red walls of a dark barn. There were no cars and no lights. I wouldn't have noticed anything if we weren't looking.

Deep down a dirt and gravel drive was a shut gate. A wooden fence corralled pale sand behind the wooden barn.

Past a thin line of trees was a wide meadow with an indent for the water I'd seen on the map. Buildings to the west could have been offices or bathrooms; I couldn't tell.

Wooden poles made up an entrance that reminded me of Clara's property, except much larger and with a sign hung at the top that read, "Tiger Bay State Forest."

"Kristen?" Marie turned off her lights as she pulled in, but the closed gate had been visible.

I jumped out and tugged for wards automatically, but there were only signs, the locked gate, and buildings with weak lights guarding the sides. Twisting Mer through the combination lock, I tweaked it open, removed the chain, and winced when the gate squeaked.

Marie rolled through quietly, and I left the gate open in case we needed to exit. She waited for me to get back in the car. The dirt road ahead looped around the buildings but branched toward the meadow to the east where our target was.

Leaving headlights off, we had little light with no moon and too many clouds. The water, a square man-made pond, reflected some light in the center. Our path dwindled to flattened grass where I worried we'd find more mud than land.

To our right, beyond the trees between the properties, there was a glint of glass reflecting the dim sky, but otherwise, I never would have known there were buildings.

We passed the water, and the road turned, circling it. Marie edged forward, tires barely grinding against sand. There was a short fence we'd have to climb over to reach the trees on the other side.

Leah spoke over the comms. "I can see the back of the house. No activity or they've got excellent blackout curtains. I can smell fumes, but that could be your car, or there were cars here recently."

"Hold," said Marie.

I leaned forward as our road straightened along the east side of the water, where elms and oaks dotted the pond's edge and thickened along the property line. There didn't seem to be much likelihood that Lambert or his cronies were at the deserted farm. We inched forward.

A Dur-Alf blasting spell threw the front of the car up two or three feet, along with a cloud of sand and gravel. Tilted, I slapped back into my seat as the engine whined, groaned, and spewed. Marie swore. When the front tires landed, my forehead smacked into the back of David's seat.

We'd gone through all the effort of sneaking in through an adjacent property, but I hadn't checked for wards yet. Our stealthy arrival had failed quite noisily.

SEVENTEEN

I started fumbling with my seatbelt when Marie barked orders. "Stay down, Leah. Report only. Kristen, light it up out there and tell me what we have."

Opening the passenger door behind her, I was halfway out while David moved quietly for the woods. An orange muzzle flash lit near the barn, and a spray of machine gun fire tore into his side of the car. I had a shield up in seconds, but I could tell by his grunt that he'd been hit. The air held that sour, sharp scent of our special ammunition.

I had a second shield blocking a binding spell aimed at me before I tossed in Haven and lit up four people in or beside the barn and attached fences.

Marie rolled over the hood ignominiously and dropped out of sight beside David, who had toppled to the ground. Widening the shield to cover them in front and me behind the car, I tossed a Dur-Alf blast where the closest witch crouched beside a fence post.

Before my spell landed, I had a second flying ten feet

behind the attacker. His fingers were digging into Dur-Alf when my spell hit.

The split pole fence shattered in wood and soil, tumbling the man back into my second blast. I had to flip two more shields up as a Mer lifting spell wove toward us like a liquid snake.

Bullets tore into all three of my shields from the two witches in the rear. They'd formed their own shields against my blast, magic glowing dull against their ghostly shapes from the Haven spell.

"David?" I asked in a whisper over the comms.

Neither of my team responded, but I could see Marie pulling David toward the car.

Refreshing my main shield, I dropped the other two. The closest witch was sidling along the barn, tossing a weak blast spell out of Dur-Alf. A woman based on her shape, she drew up a shield of her own.

My detection spell did not reach the house behind the barn, nor the forest where Leah hid. When Leah spoke over the comms, I guessed her to be about an equal distance from the road, on the other side of the property in thin woods. "I've got movement at a house window. There's light inside, or was, and they just moved a curtain."

"Be careful; they might be using Haven to spot you." If I were them, I would be checking the rear.

"Kristen, get over here." Marie had moved to the front of the car.

One of the guns stopped firing bursts, but the witch didn't move. The woman had nearly joined the man at the corner. They had to have vehicles. I searched for a hint of one or more as I sprang for the front of the car. Its tires flat, it had sunk to the ground and stunk of radiator fluid and oil.

Following my movement, a binding spell spun toward the edge of my wide shield, forcing me to throw another up to block it. These witches had a hard time maintaining two spells.

"Marie," I said as I rounded the bent grill and buckled hood. Back to me, she was kneeling beside David, who was pale in the darkness and grimacing. I saw no signs of blood or rips in his vest.

"Wrap a tight shield around David, and leave it. We're moving forward." She didn't say he'd been hurt, but obviously we wouldn't leave him behind and protected if he weren't.

Bullets resumed a heavy barrage against my shield, and I added a second layer to it. The special ammunition ate into it quicker than normal gunfire. David had dark wet spots from two shots in his right leg. If the metal were inside him, it would continue to poison him.

"Sorry." Trickling out two lifting spells from Mer, modified to nearly unlocking spells, I dug blue streams into the gunshot wounds. The sparkling darkness of the Tarus realm misted around David. Leyna had used the spell on a ricochet stuck in a hunter. This was my first time to try it on anyone, let alone a vampire.

He stiffened, then relaxed immediately as I dug through for metal. The wound in his upper thigh had a bullet wedged against bone. I whipped the ball of metal to the grass. The second had gone through his calf.

Marie nodded, still leaning forward, ready to attack. She only saw the bullet pop out, I assumed. Who knew what dragons saw of magic?

The gunfire paused, and three concerted blasting spells tore at our location. Leaving one shield in front of us and one covering David, I met all three with a weak but concave shield that focused most of the blast outward. I still spit out grass and soil.

"Ready?" she asked. "I need to be within about ten yards."

That meant we needed to cover half the distance, which would put us into the trees. Of the four defenders, three were active. The man who I'd hit with two blasting spells hadn't moved.

The woman attempting to retreat had nearly reached the shield of the witch firing from the left corner of the barn, a man from his build and stance. "One sec," I said.

I threw the blasting spell first — at his shield. Once it left my hand, I let it continue undirected. The binding spell I threw a second later and aimed for two steps behind her.

"Hurry. We're going to lose them if they delay us too much longer. They're keeping us out here." Marie had her weapon ready, and I believed she would shoot them given the opportunity. "Leah, any movement outside?" she asked.

"Nothing."

My blasting spell passed wide of the woman, and the Dur-Alf explosion slammed into the man's shield, blowing splinters and a hidden camera off the barn and gutters. It equally lurched the woman forward as it washed into her from behind.

Her shield dropped in surprise or pain, and I slipped a binding spell around her. "Go," I said reluctantly. A rash charge like this might keep the shooter from aiding the bound witch, or it would get us killed.

Throwing two shields far ahead of us, I covered us from both shooters while the female witch slapped to the ground. I barely kept up with Marie as she fired once and dashed.

The glint of glass alerted me to a security camera at

the corner, aimed toward the entrance. "Leah, security cameras."

In any enforcement activity, we never would have charged in so recklessly. However, once Marie's tail snapped out of golden Salmhalla, crossed ten yards in a flash, and thrashed the shooter ahead of us, I felt better about running into the fray.

The farthest shooter to the right darted behind the barn, and I threw a fresh Haven spell deeper into the yard. It wasn't strong enough to light up anyone in the house. "I still have just the three active. One possibly injured. One bound."

I tugged another binding spell as Marie's tail retreated, leaving the shooter and his weapon scattered and exposed beside the barn. Before he could shake himself to alertness, I slipped a tight bind around him. "Two bound." The third retreated toward the house slowly. "Last shooter backing toward the house. I've got nothing else."

As we approached the woman bound on the ground with my spell, Marie shifted, head panning from one side to the next. Her jaw was tight, and her eyebrows drew down in a fierce glower. "Leah, any movement at the house from your position?"

"None. Cameras, though."

"Move in a little. Be careful." Marie sidled to the left to go around the man bound by my spell. Gunfire rattled into the shield I had in front of her.

Stressed, my fingers pinched tightly to tug at the realms, searching for wards as she slowed. Blues and greens rippled at my side, but the stretch of driveway between us and the house remained dark. In the pale light of the clouds, two bay doors of a garage faced us with only a hint at the side of the house closer to where I imagined Leah approached. I didn't trust that it would be easy to reach the building.

As Marie stepped forward, I flicked a Haven spell toward the exposed house and replaced the shield. Faint wisps marked movement deep inside the building. Her tail whipped out toward the brighter shape of the last witch firing at us.

Her tail hit him hard, as if to cleave him in half. Instead, he folded around it, and when he landed near the house over twenty yards away, I hit him with a binding spell.

"Too easy," I said more to myself than anyone else.

Marie stalked toward the house over the drive, aiming at the bay doors rather than the back. "Leah, where are you?"

"I've got you in sight. To your right." She didn't show up in my Haven detection spell, so I tossed one toward the back of the house that splashed against the wall.

I found Leah, a faint glimmer of stalking white in the thin woods to our right. The only other movement scurried deep inside at the opposite corner of the house from us. They had cameras at the corner of the garage and over the front door.

"There's no one close." I gestured to the house for Marie. "Far rear corner."

Without a reply, Marie sprinted to the left of the garage. I pushed our shield out ahead of her and frantically tugged at the realms to search for traps.

The flash deep at the back of the property was from the same weapon they'd used to breech Clara's house. I yanked a shield toward it, but the missile moved quick as a bullet — faster than my spell. "Marie!"

I misjudged. Marie flicked forward out of its path while my shields were useless and trailing behind her, with nothing to stop the missile from hitting the side of the garage in front of me. Twenty feet away, I caught the brunt of the explosion as it blasted wood shards in all directions and threw me ass-first onto the driveway.

My shields were lost with the impact. I flinched as gunfire sounded from deep in the back of the property. My ears rang from the explosion, but I could make out two automatic weapons as I flung a hasty shield to my left side.

Clara and Bea had to be here, considering the force protecting the house and barn. Our overzealous charge had been worse than risky. "Marie?"

Flames tonguing out of the side of the garage lit the front steps of the house in dancing shadows. Only Haven gave me a glimpse of Marie smashing through the front door. We were reacting at a disadvantage.

Bullets tore at my shield and the asphalt at the edges of my spell. My hand trembled as I reached for Dur-Alf.

"Get clear, Kristen." Marie's tail whipped out of golden Salmhalla and snapped inside the dark house.

Splinters tugged at my skin and flesh along my legs and right arm. I bled from my chin and cheek, but I was surprisingly intact for my proximity to the explosion. "Got it."

Growling under my breath, I replaced my tattering shield and lobbed two Dur-Alf blasting spells toward the muzzle flashes in the dark shadows at the back of the property. Splinters of wood pried painfully between my sleeve and where they'd embedded into my skin. A particularly sharp piece dug into my right thigh when I rolled to my knees. I could make for the front door as well as anywhere else, and probably should.

My blasting spells hit just in time as the grenade launcher fired again. This time, it angled steeply into the ground not five yards from where it was launched. Dirt and debris rained upward around the fireball.

"I'm at the house, Pyre. Breech?" Leah's voice was sharp over the comms.

"Negative. Circle toward the back, but be careful."

"Got it, Pyre."

I yanked a shard of wood from my thigh, exposing an inch of the tip wet with my blood, before I staggered to my feet. Gunfire had stopped at the back of the property, but I lobbed a blasting spell into those trees just in case. Before it went off, I had a second shield up, curving from the left side to my front.

Marie had disappeared into the darkness inside.

Two steps toward the door, I tossed a Haven detection spell inside. "Heading in behind you, Marie." She lit up, moving slowly deeper, and three shapes were exiting the back side. "I've got three coming out the back, Leah. House is clear, Marie." Either Clara and Bea had never been here, or they were being whisked away from us now.

Tired and shaky, I tugged at the realms, searching for wards. I found nothing and stepped inside despite leaving armed threats behind us. Shifting one of the shields, I blocked the front entry.

It was pitch black inside, except for the sharp white outlines of Marie as she strode away from me. The three who had been exiting were running in a straight line away from me, growing dimmer in Haven's light.

"Marie?" I asked over the comms. She was already crossing through a room beyond the front living room. "What's your plan?"

"Follow them."

I would rather be outside than trapped in the house if the jerks with the rocket launcher were still active. A stalking ghost appeared at the back as Leah grew nearer.

We were rushing into a group who had been quite willing to set traps and use conventional weapons. "We need to be careful." My entire right side hurt from the blast.

"Pyre, I can smell them. They were here. Bea and Clara." Leah spoke quietly, crouched at the back of the house.

"Finn. Backup?" Marie asked.

"Two local FBI, Pyre. Fifteen minutes out. I've got four more gearing up, but they were off-duty."

"Cold sands. Tomas, whatever surveillance you can get out here. I think we're too late and out-gunned." She was nearly at the back door, and so was Leah.

I stumbled in the dark through what might be a living room. Tired from using so much magic and wounded from the blast, the toe of my boot caught something, and I dropped to my knees. Grinding my shin on a limb, I rolled to my left side and forward, planting a hand onto a cool, crushed chest. The hint of broken ribs had my pulse rising and stomach twisting.

Scrambling, I began to smell the blood and more. "Marie. I've got a body." Maybe she'd killed someone when she first entered. No, it hadn't been warm.

EIGHTEEN

y racing pulse doubled when I imagined Clara or Bea dead beside me. Splinters or not, I was on my feet before Marie swore. "Who is it?" she asked.

I grimaced at the possibility of finding one or both of them dead and fumbled at my belt for my flashlight. Instead, the interrupting hail of gunfire breaking windows to my left had me flicking up a fresh shield. Fluttering curtains let in some light, but I only caught splintering wood from a polished dining room table ahead of them.

In Haven, I could make out Marie and Leah both crouching at the back of the house. There had to be three guns firing at the house from the amount of damage they caused. My shield caught a number of the bullets, but I'd left Leah and Marie unprotected.

I winced at the thought, but the body could wait. Stumbling forward, I made out a kitchen with a back door where Marie had exited. She and Leah were the only white shapes in my Haven vision, so our attackers had to be deep in the back of the property.

Glass shattered inside cabinets as I pulled a Dur-Alf shield and whipped it out the doorway over Marie's head. My first shield was thinning from the gunfire, and likely special ammo, but I focused on making a second one outside to help cover Leah.

"Three semi-automatics, and they're moving deeper into the woods. What's northeast of our location, Finn?"

"A trail or drive, Pyre, then acres of forest. The trail meets up with a road to your west and appears to lead back toward the highway about a mile east."

I refreshed my own shield and moved closer to the back door and my team. The night sky lit the sparse forest behind the house and a split fence similar to the one in front. Marie and Leah were well protected by my shield, but the house was slowly being shredded. I crouched at the doorway, peering around the corner at muzzle flashes deep in the woods.

The thought of them sending a grenade into the house behind me made me shudder. David was unprotected back at the car, and I'd left too many hostiles behind us. One witch could unbind the others.

"Two vehicles, Pyre. Pickup trucks, I believe." Leah's voice was low over the splintering and shattering sounds behind me. I certainly couldn't hear engines over the bullets.

"Where?" Marie rose, but my shield protected her. The shooters weren't focused on them, but the house.

"Pulling behind the guns, Pyre. Heading west if I'm right." With Leah's hearing, she wouldn't be wrong.

"Move it. Kristen, keep us shielded." Marie lunged toward the gunfire, leaving me scrambling to add a fourth shield, fresh and thick, in her path and keeping pace with her.

I dropped my shield and hopped onto the ground to

follow behind Leah. Juggling three shields taxed my already sagging strength. Breathing deeply, I dragged in the sour scent of special ammo. The rhythm of gunfire shifted, and I guessed someone reloaded.

Haven detection lit up Marie ahead, climbing over a split fence. It wasn't my spell, so one of the witches had to have set it in case we rushed them.

The gunfire shifted quickly, tearing into the shield I'd made for her, and where the bullets missed that, they hit mine and Leah's. A Dur-Alf blast shot toward her, and I pushed her shield toward it and prepped another to replace it.

I could hear the trucks grumbling through the woods. They hadn't turned on their headlights.

The blast blew apart the split rail fence and sent white sand and grass into the air, but Marie only stumbled. She had her weapon out but wasn't trying to aim through my shields. Leah was a pace away, gaining as the fence didn't block her way. I was slowing and a good twenty feet behind.

The witches' Haven spell marked our attackers faintly, and I could see one turning and running away while the other two continued firing. The scent of fire had me checking over my shoulder to the garage, but the flames were gone.

"Not going to make it, Pyre. One's already taking off at full speed." Leah adjusted her course, darting behind Marie and angling to the left.

As she spoke, the red lights of a pickup truck lit, and headlights flooded the trees behind the property where we'd left David. The second vehicle was a shadow with an occasional glint, picking up the shooters one-by-one.

I jogged to a near stop and strained to pull a blasting spell out of Dur-Alf. Higher up, as if they were standing in the back of a truck, gunfire rained toward us. I aimed a good ten feet ahead of the muzzle flashes.

The second shooter had climbed in when my explosion brought the satisfying sound of glass shattering and perhaps metal buckling. The engine roared, despite my attempt, and the third witch firing at us blurred under the Haven spell.

Marie and Leah were only thirty feet from the truck, with my tattered shields barely protecting them, when the sounds of tires digging in sand announced the witches racing down the dirt road.

"Drop the shields!" Marie yelled. She began firing as I did so, and Leah joined her. Bullets clanged on metal, but the truck didn't slow.

There was one burst of return fire before their red tail-lights disappeared behind trees. We had no vehicle to pursue them.

I made it two more trembling steps before my strength gave way and I dropped to a knee. Marie and Leah were a hazy pair of ghosts in the woods.

We'd been close, but Lambert and his witches had been prepared. Who lay dead in the house? Bea? Clara? Both of them? I doubted they had gotten whatever information they wanted from Clara that quickly. Bea was dead. We'd risked too much and failed.

"Tomas, find them. Track them. Do not lose them."

"Yes, Pyre." His high-pitch was unsure and resigned. In the city, he might have video feeds and traffic cams to work with, but not here. Slightly more optimistic, he continued. "I've locked onto some phones from that location starting yesterday evening. They might offer some leads. Most appear to be discarded in the area, so they won't help me with tracking Lambert."

"Thanks, Tomas. Who was it in the house, Kristen?"

Drained, I was breathing heavy. "Didn't get a chance to see." Part of me didn't want to know who we'd find crushed on the floor.

"You okay?" she asked. Her shape approached me in the pale light of the dwindling Haven spell.

"Yeah. Better than David." And whoever was in the house. I hated that I hoped it was some innocent home-owner rather than Bea. She'd been so vibrant.

"Oh, I'm just slacking back here." His voice was slow and tired.

"Help's on the way," said Finn quietly over the comms. Knowing Finn, we'd have a dwarf on scene soon enough to heal David and the rest of us.

I pushed myself up and spoke as Marie approached with Leah trailing. "Let me make sure there are no wards we haven't found. We should check on the four at the barn. One of them wasn't bound."

"Agreed." Marie bled along the side of her bald scalp. Her eyes flicked across the blood stains on my pants and sleeve, then toward the garage and barn. "I'll want to talk to them."

Turning toward the house, I tugged at the realms, and once I was sure we didn't have a ward waiting for us, threw a Haven detection spell to the barn.

Four prone bodies waited for us. I'd want to bind the man who I'd hit with a blasting spell. As fanatical as this coven appeared to be, I doubted any would yield to a simple interrogation.

Marie walked beside me, keeping to my slower pace. "You did well."

"We should have checked for wards in the adjoining property. If we had, we might have had a chance to sneak up on them."

Her head cocked slightly, then she nodded. "Perhaps.

We didn't have the manpower. Finn, when does Mika arrive with their team?"

"Still on schedule for 10:11 a.m., Pyre."

The scent of smoldering wood mixed with spent gunpowder and sharp hints of chemical explosives. I plucked at splinters I could find, but most had been either yanked out or snapped off under my clothes.

The amount of energy I'd expended on magic had me nearly shaking with fatigue. I needed liquid and food, and more than a little rest.

I flushed with guilt. Someone, I knew it was Bea, was dead inside that house. Lambert had Clara. From how he'd killed Phillip and attempted to do with Tomas, the witch was a monster. If Iliodor had sent him, then I understood why Marie wanted to stop him.

The witches I'd bound were still alert, but trapped. With a raised eyebrow, I checked with Marie at the first in case she wanted me to modify the binding so they could speak.

She shook her head. "They can wait. I want to see what we have going on inside."

The spells were hardy and vibrant, as I expected. A person could die of dehydration before the spell degraded if no one interfered. Without comment, I sent pictures of their faces to Tomas. I was too tired for his snide remarks. We took a lap around the barn, and I inspected each before sending quick photos.

The man I'd caught between two blasting spells was alive but unresponsive. Still, I wrapped him in a binding spell and left him unconscious.

As we circled back and passed the gutted garage, Marie lit her flashlight; Leah and I followed suit. I swallowed apprehension as Marie stepped inside the front door, with her light bathing a black leather couch. Tufts of padding sprouted out of several bullet holes. The furniture and sparse the decor appeared to have been moderately expensive.

She flicked on a switch beside the door, and yellow light shone from a ceiling fan.

There were soda cans on the coffee table, liquid dripping to the floor, and plenty of bullet holes in the walls. The north window had a tattered lavender curtain and glass scattered from the sill to the middle of the living room rug.

"Clara and Bea were here. I can smell them." Leah clicking her flashlight off reminded me to do the same. I could see where she'd shredded her outfit in the woods, and burrs clung heavily to her pants. Of the four of us, she'd come out of this in the best shape.

Somberly, Marie led the march to the dining room, a quiet funeral procession.

Bea had been crushed by a Dur-Alf spell. Her lively smile gone forever, her face was distorted with broken cheek and jaw bones. Blood from her eyes and ears matted her golden curls. Her clothes were stained and sunken with her body where bones had yielded to the spell.

My expression ranged from a grimace to a snarl as my emotions rolled from sadness to disgust and ended in rage. I'd seen David and Marie broken with shattered bones, but they'd accepted the dangers of our job.

Lambert, or one of his coven, had murdered Bea. They could have easily bound her and left her for someone to find.

"Why?" I asked.

"Perhaps he's just the type of human who likes to kill," said Marie. The tinge of sadness in her voice, and the terminology, made me remember she was not human.

The dining room had taken plenty of damage, though

most was waist high, so Bea's corpse hadn't been shot. It didn't make it any better.

"Monitors for the cameras." I stepped beside two shattered monitors knocked off the dining room table that added the slight scent of hot plastic to the room. Alongside was a less damaged piece of equipment. "Police band monitor."

"We need something that will tell us where they went," said Marie. Her tone had hardened, but not at me.

There was a hall leading to the right, where I guessed bedrooms and bathrooms were. "I'm checking the other rooms." Instinctively, I tugged at the realms to search for wards while I left the others behind. I couldn't stare at Bea's ruined face.

Marie appeared as though she might say something, then let me go.

"All four witches you've got there are out of Texas, Pyre. Connected to the other two at the hotel. Sending names and profiles."

I didn't pause to let her drag me out to question them. In my mood, I'd want to hurt them as some revenge for Bea. Instead, I flicked on lights, scanning for a quick detail. From the lack of belongings or even decor, no one appeared to actually live here. One of the bedrooms had signs of having been occupied, with rumpled covers where someone might have napped. On a dark cherry bureau, a closed laptop was charging on the otherwise unused top.

The device in hand, I returned to find Leah and Marie searching cabinets and a sideboard. "Think we can get anything from this?"

Leah flashed a smile and pointed to a broken cell phone placed on the dining room table. "If it's better shape than that."

"Tomas, we've got a laptop," Marie said as she nodded to me.

I avoided looking at Bea, then forced myself to. She didn't deserve to be ignored and forgotten. It wasn't right. I'd only known her for a couple of hours more than Clara.

"I'll work with Leah on it, Pyre."

My lips puckered in a frown, but I passed over the equipment. I refused to say anything.

Marie nudged her chin toward the open door. "Let's go see if anyone would like to talk." I shrugged and followed.

Somehow, losing Bea had taken some of the urgency out of chasing Lambert. I stiffened and focused on the Marie's back. I was getting frustrated and punchy over the brutality in Lambert's wake.

Finn cleared his throat. Had he noticed Tomas's slight? "Pyre, two agents pulling up to the front. What are their orders?"

"Have them hold, Finn. How long before we have transports and medical?"

"A little over thirty for medical; they had to retrieve supplies for David. Less than an hour to secure transport for the witches you captured."

We strode out into air that was less fresh than the house due to the smoldering garage, but less stifling than being inside with Bea's corpse.

"Tomas, any leads from their phone activity?" Marie asked.

"No, Pyre. I can track activity pretty straightforward from either Texas or Alabama. No deviations that would give me another location. All burners. They are probably heading out of the city."

"Finn?" Marie asked, though I couldn't be sure what she expected from him.

"I've got nearly all airports on lockdown and locals

heading to the International Speedway Boulevard now with orders to look for trucks, Pyre. APB on trucks. No approach orders. I have traffic jams on I-95 and I-4 in progress from Consociation support teams. If Lambert gets Clara on the highway, I'll stall them there. I've got images of all members of Lambert's coven distributed, as well as Clara. There's little I can do other than APBs on other local roads."

"Sounds good." Marie's tone was flat and distracted, considering what he'd put into motion.

I was surprised, but Finn and Marie had worked together long enough, he knew their procedures. I'd barely survived a few cases. His position as support back at the office made me realize how badly his predecessor, Stacey, had hampered our cases.

My lips tightened, but I spoke anyway. "If it is Iliodor, he probably knows your default procedures."

Marie eyed me as we crossed the driveway. "Perhaps. Suggestions? Alternatives?"

"Unfortunately, no." We couldn't cordon off the entire county. I sighed and focused on our closest witch. Something had to break, or we'd never find Clara. We'd been lucky to guess Lambert would come here with her after Alabama, but luck wasn't going to save Clara.

CHAPTER
NINETEEN

I swapped the binding spell for one that left the man some control of his head and vocal cords, but he just glowered. Marie said nothing as she knelt and roughly searched his pockets. His eyes widened when their contact showed him Salmhalla. His awe lasted seconds before his silent glare returned.

Cars passed on the highway at the front of the property. I heard a semi and a couple heavier engines that could have been pickup trucks.

Marie found nothing but a burner phone until she checked his neck and head and came out with comms that looped over his ear. She listened to it, then tucked it in her pocket. If we could get it to the office, we might have a link to Lambert. This crew was smart; they'd know we had their people.

"Name?" she asked him, but we already had a list with photos.

His lips tightened, blatantly refusing to speak.

She cocked her head toward the woman lying near the front of the barn. The witch had auburn hair tied into a ponytail that had snarled, and when she could speak, she swore. "Consociation lackey. You should be working for freedom for our powers. You're a betrayal to all witches."

The few covens I'd been involved with wouldn't agree. Most considered the Consociation heavy-handed, but necessary to avoid the witch hunts the general populace would perpetuate. I ignored the woman and left for the other side of the barn while Marie searched her.

After a question from Tomas to Leah, their comms went silent, separated from the group as they worked on the laptop. Hopefully, something would come from it.

The man I'd slammed with dual blasting spells still appeared unconscious. His breathing was regular, but his pulse was thready. I winced as I pressed fingers deep into his neck. "How soon will we have medical? I knocked a witch out with blasting spells, and he's in rough shape."

He had a thin beard, the five-day shadow kind, and bruises showed along his right cheek and temple. Despite the fact he'd been trying to shoot us, and possibly had put bullets into David, I didn't want to kill him. I flushed when Lambert came to mind and the emotions that accompanied the thoughts.

"Still a while out. David will be priority."

"I appreciate that. Feeling a bit better as it is, but thirsty." David's voice sounded tired, and his attempted lilt at the end wilted.

I stood up from the unconscious witch and glanced back for Marie, but she was still on the other side. "I'm sure they'll be here soon, David."

Hoping he'd survive, I left the man stretched on white sand with pieces of fence strewn about and headed for the last witch at the back. My binding spell had caught him oddly, with one leg stretched out and the other bent so that he lay on his side.

As I reached him, an SUV pulled over on the highway outside the gate. "Local FBI here?" I reached for Dur-Alf wearily, too tired to handle another attack.

"Should be pulling up out front."

I sighed and relaxed.

The last Texan witch was older, with gray at his temples and a nearly white mustache. His jaw tightened when I replaced his binding spell, but he refused to speak. He did try and search the area he could see. When he saw the other man, he swore, and his eyes tightened into a glare at me.

I watched a man and woman in black suits step out of the SUV and attentively peer into the dark yard. Smoke still drifted from the garage, but that was all they would really see from their position.

The yard we'd crossed recklessly seemed a shorter distance than it had during the commotion. I'd seen Marie dive into danger a few times, but this morning had come close to blind foolishness. In the end, we'd have done better focusing on the exits and containing them, but I wasn't about to mention it. Maybe Clara had played a part in Marie's decision. The memory of touching Bea's crushed body made me shiver.

"Marie, I'm going to check on David, okay?" I doubted we'd get anything from these witches, not even their names.

"Go ahead."

Stinging from the splinters stuck under my clothes, I was digging through vines and brush with our damaged vehicle and David in sight when Tomas spoke excitedly over the comms. "We've got something, Pyre."

"What?" she asked.

I paused, peering back where she straightened over the

older male witch. Exhaustion fought with excitement. Saving Clara was almost second to stopping Lambert.

"This laptop has been active from another location for three weeks. I'm trying to get exact details, but Finn's getting the access for me. Right now, I know where it's been, down to the apartment number. I can say there's no internet activity from the location at the present, but that's all."

"Where?" Marie's voice held little optimism.

"In the city, Pyre. Sending address now. A development called Pelican Bay."

Letting out a slow breath, I retreated out of the brush and marched toward Marie. I doubted they'd want to head into Finn's net, if they knew DRC procedure. They'd be on back roads out of the area.

"They won't head there," Marie said.

I smiled weakly to myself. None of us would expect them anywhere but blazing a trail out of the county. As organized as they'd been, they probably had replacement vehicles waiting.

"Leah, Kristen, head out to the apartment and check. Maybe we'll find something they left behind. Tomas, work on what they were using the laptop for. Finn, get a vehicle from the local FBI for Leah and Kristen."

"Got it, Pyre." Finn's voice cut off sharply from the comms.

Glancing toward the road, I still ambled toward Marie. Guilt flushed at my cheeks when I considered a stop at a coffee shop or gas station. Bea was dead, David wounded, and Clara was with this beast Lambert. It wasn't entirely selfish; I needed something to bolster my sagging energy.

We still hadn't located Oscar, or even determined his full involvement. "Has there been any activity on Manny or his wife?" Perhaps Oscar and the couple had been part of the crew here.

"Nothing," said Finn. "Their cell phones have remained at the house ever since you followed them there last night."

I hadn't needed to ask. If Tomas or Finn found any clues from the couple, Oscar, or the attackers at the hotel, we would have known immediately. At least, once the firefight here had calmed down.

The dull rumble of a helicopter sounded in the west, but I didn't see any lights in the night sky. Marie glanced over the horizon as well. "Finn, you got helicopters in the air?"

"One, Pyre. Just arrived out of DeLand. I have them searching for westbound traffic on the highway near you. Then we'll check a north side road."

Leah jogged out, laptop in hand. "We got time to grab my bag?" she asked Marie.

Appraising the older man on the ground, Marie waved us toward David and the ruined car.

I sighed and turned back toward the bramble and trees between the property, but I did have snacks in my go bag.

We strode toward the property line. Leah sniffed. "You get hit? I can smell your blood."

Waving a speckled shirt sleeve in the air, I explained, "Shrapnel. Splinters. This is the bad one." I pointed to my thigh. "You?"

"I've ruined the blouse." Leah flashed a smile. "Finn's not going to like paying to replace it."

I nearly stumbled, cocking my head. "You can expense the clothes?"

David chuckled over the comms. "Newbie. You think I can afford to go through these suits?"

"Finn?" I asked incredulously.

"It's in our budget. We're not the FBI. Tomas would have sent you the benefits package early on."

I paused for Tomas to make a snarky remark about my ineptitude, but he didn't. I'd been focused on the medical and likely missed that part. There would be a file of my receipts from now on.

We pushed through the vegetation toward David, with Leah holding the laptop above her shoulder. Tomas had said the burner phones were left on the property. They obviously considered them expendable with no clues to offer. "Was the laptop locked?" I asked. The iPad hadn't been.

"Yes." Leah winced as branches snagged in her blond hair.

"The iPad. If we hadn't found the codenames, we wouldn't have led them to Clara."

Marie spoke over the comms. "You think it's a trap?"

I frowned, not sure of my concerns. "Misdirection at least. If it had been unlocked, I'd be more confident it was."

"Be careful."

Most likely, they wanted us looking elsewhere. Then again, Lambert was brutal. "I plan to be."

CHAPTER
TWENTY

When we reached David, I released the shield I'd locked over him. His face was pale. The wounds on his leg weren't bleeding, or at least the blood on his pants was drying, but he didn't do more than shift his head. His tin of mints was in his hand.

"How do you feel?" I asked.

"Like I'm a month off my last feeding." He smiled wide enough to show his sharp cuspids. "I'm just letting my body heal itself, but I'll need something to work with soon." He was being serious, and that worried me.

"We missed you." Leah kicked his shoe playfully as she passed him on her way to the back door of the car. "Got a little nasty."

"I heard." His face remained handsome, even when a light frown crossed his face. "I didn't enjoy being sidelined, and now I'll have to deal with a dwarf."

"Sorry you have to stoop so low."

David chuckled. "That's bad. I'll have to tell that one when they get here."

Leah tossed my bag out of the back of the car. "Don't encourage her." She held my purse with her bags.

Finn spoke over the comms. "You're go on the vehicle. They are not happy to lose their bucar. Pyre's off comms while she interviews the witches. Let us know if you need her."

I'd heard the nickname "bucar" for bureau cars before, from actual agents. Many ended up with vehicles for months. I could understand them being annoyed. Usually we got one from their motor pool, not one personally assigned.

"Feel better, David." I took my purse when Leah offered it.

"Give me a few pints, and I'll catch up."

We left David and walked straight for the highway rather than cut through the thin line of trees. I hoped we weren't walking into a trap, but the leads were getting cold. The longer it was between Lambert racing away with Clara and not getting an alert from local enforcement, the more likely we were to have lost them.

"Lambert's probably going to change vehicles." I made the statement mostly for Finn.

I wasn't surprised when he answered. "Agreed. At this point, I'm searching for damaged, abandoned trucks just to point me in the right direction."

The male agent at the black Nissan Pathfinder attempted to hide his glower while the woman had an amused smirk. I assumed it was his bucar. The plastic bag stuffed with belongings at his feet confirmed my belief.

"Sorry," Leah said. "Keys inside?"

"Yeah. It's low on gas." He had the pinched kind of face that made me glad he didn't try and smile.

The woman's eyes widened when we got close enough

for her to see what rough shape we were in. I offered a weak smile as I opened the passenger door. "Thanks."

Leah slid the laptop on the floor behind my seat before settling behind the wheel. I tossed my bag and purse at my feet as she started the engine. "Shame we need to stop for gas," she said.

"Damned shame." Buckled in, I pulled up my go bag for a pair of protein bars. I tossed her a bar, unwrapped mine, and stuck it between my teeth to pull up directions. I pointed her east, opposite of where we were parked.

"You okay? Seemed to take Bea's death hard." Leah pulled us onto the quiet highway and through the median to head west. As we bounced vigorously, I imagined the pinch-faced man's expression.

"Yeah." I took a bite and chewed thoughtfully. "She was nice. I think there's some guilt there too. I initially questioned if she was the one who leaked the location."

Leah nodded, steering with her knees while opening her bar. I adjusted the map to avoid I-95 and Finn's blocks. The blueberry lemon had me wishing we'd grabbed water. We'd passed a Race Trac on the trip west and would be able to stop there.

We were driving by a housing development on our left when I finished my snack. I was still beat from wielding so much magic, but it helped. "Who's Mika?"

"Merfolk. I worked with them a couple of times. About as opposite to Pyre as you get. You'd think they didn't take the job seriously, but they're sharp and quick. Great at illusion magic."

"They? Nonbinary?"

"Yep. They'll have some kind of wild hair color, but they can zip that into brown or black in a flash. Tattooed to the gills, pun intended." Leah smiled, watching the road. "You'll get along. Everyone gets along with Mika."

"David?"

"Oh, he moans, but loves them. Mika flirts with him and leaves him hanging. It's fun to watch."

We passed a wide-load truck with half a house on it. My first thought was what a great disguise *that* would be to hide Clara. Lambert had the advantage at this point. APBs couldn't cover every exit from the county. If he'd headed west to DeLand, there were more roads and options to lose us.

"Well, there might be nothing for them to do when they get here."

"True. I've got faith in Tomas and Finn, though." She mocked a shocked expression and pointed to her comms.

I flushed. "I wish they had more to work with." We weren't going to find anything at the apartment.

TWENTY-ONE

At the gas station, I opted for several variations of cheese and bread to build up my strength. The day-old pizza tucked in cardboard I ate first, despite the pleasant man at the counter who suggested fresh slices would be available in half an hour.

I went with bottled coffees out of consideration for the agent's bucar. "Five minutes," I mumbled when I had the map up on my phone. Even a little food brought my energy up.

"I think you just dripped cheese on his seat." Leah smirked so I couldn't tell if she was teasing.

We were both covered in burrs and dirt anyway. "Can he expense a car detail through the DRC?"

It took us five minutes to turn into the complex that had a country club feel, and two honks of the horn to get the gate attendant to wake up.

The apartment we were sent to check was in a massive development with expensive row houses along meandering streets. No one was moving at this hour except an athletic jogger and an older man in sweats smoking on his lawn.

His gray puff of a dog bounced at his feet as we passed. A country club sign marked a side road between palm trees.

The address led to expansive quads with three floors and parking on the street rather than garages. Maybe it wasn't as posh as it first appeared.

"146C." I pointed to the empty reserved parking space. "Upstairs, maybe?" I considered a Haven detection spell, but if we were dealing with witches they might be awake and see it.

Leah crawled past. "A, B, and D are taken. One guest car." There were three sedans and one mini Mazda SUV. She parked across the road in a guest spot. "I'm guessing Clara is not here."

"Unlikely." I unbuckled slowly, scanning the well-lit neighborhood. There were plenty of planted areas, but few that could conceal an ambush of more than one person. Stepping out of the car, I studied the building we were to investigate.

All the front lights were on, and the short streetlamp behind us cast our shadows across the road. A couple of the windows had glows behind curtains, some slightly bluish from televisions. The windows I assumed were the upstairs apartment we'd be searching were all dark.

Leah walked to the first car parked in front of the building, and then the next. When she glanced at me, I cocked my head questioningly.

"They're cold. Haven't been driven." She touched her nose.

The air was fresh to me. Perhaps a touch of exhaust in the breeze from our SUV. While she checked the vehicles, I tugged at the realms, searching for wards, then approached the door through a sidewalk between hedges. The window directly overhead had no curtains and no hint of light.

A sidelite decorated the front entrance, and I could see

stairs that led up to a dark room. I tugged at the realms and again considered a Haven detection spell, but unlocked the door with Mer instead.

"It's odd," Leah said quietly. "No wards?"

"None."

"You'd think a group of witches would have something."

I did too. At least, this group would. Retrieving my flashlight off my belt, I lit the stairs through the side window. "Well, we might be setting off a conventional alarm. Let me go first. Shielded."

Leah shrugged and took a step back.

I formed the shield close to my body, curving at the sides and over my head. When it was thick enough to handle a Dur-Alf blasting spell, I slid a lifting spell around it to push open the door. Nobody fired, and a blast didn't throw me back into Leah, so I tugged at the realms again and stepped inside.

The explosion of fire came from my left side and slapped me so hard against the opposite wall that I dropped my flashlight. Liquid flames splashed off my shield and out the doorway toward Leah.

The impact dazed me, but not enough to lose my control of the shield. My pulse pounded in my neck, and I sucked in hot air as I drew the spell tightly around myself.

Finn heard some of the roar over the comms. "Leah? Kristen?"

I stepped back instinctively. My shoulders slapped against the narrow window, and my breath hitched. Orange blinded me from all sides. I pressed my fingers to the wall behind as panic grew tight in my chest. Feeling too trapped, I held my breath and didn't answer Finn. The heat burned at my shield, seeping in with a promise of incinerating me.

Closing my eyes, I spun my back around the frame and staggered out and onto the sidewalk. With cool darkness ahead, I could see. The door was on fire, and Leah patted at her singed clothing and hair.

I threw another shield between us and the house, then stumbled past her. She caught my elbow, and the dark mist of Ya Keya blossomed about her as we stepped away from the inferno.

As the flames roared inside, I realized there had been little noise from the firebomb. As quickly as it had released fire, it had barely made a popping sound. "We need to get everyone out," I said. "Tomas, Finn, we set off a firebomb."

"You knock. I'll blow the car horn." Leah leaped for our car.

Fire lit the front of the building like daylight as flames ate at the top of the door frame and reached the upper window. Scampering around the hedges, I dragged my shield with me as I made for the apartment below the one we'd just ignited.

As I slipped into the inset entrance to the bottom apartment, I heard Leah scuff on the asphalt of the parking lot. Even as I pounded on the door, I glanced behind.

She'd fallen just short of the back of the Pathfinder. My knocking slowed after the second as I realized she lay oddly stiff instead of rising. A Dur-Alf binding spell glowed around her, almost hidden by the bright flames and flickering shadows.

Already panicked from the firebomb, I jerked back against the door. A binding spell splashed across the wall beside me as I yanked my shield close to me.

Two Dur-Alf blasts shredded the hedges out front, buffeting against my shield. I was weak from the earlier encounter, slightly singed, and facing at least three witches. My partner was exposed in the street.

TWENTY-TWO

I pulled my weapon and tossed a Haven detection spell to the street. "We've been ambushed, Finn."

"I've got local FBI fifteen minutes out. Local police are eight minutes out. Pyre and David are awaiting transport to your location."

"Leah's bound in the middle of the parking lot."

"Crap. Hold on, I've got support coming."

Three more Dur-Alf blasts nearly ate my shield. Marked by Haven, one white ghostly form approached from across the parking lot.

The locks on the door I was leaning against clicked. "FBI. Exit out the back," I yelled.

As I formed a new shield and dropped my battered one, I fired through a small hole toward the closest witch. I didn't expect to hit them, but hoped it warned the occupants not to open the door and escape as I suggested.

"I've got three attacking from the east."

The shredded brush gave an earthy spice to the air, with only hints of smoke from the burning building. My second gunshot convinced the witch to back away from Leah and the resident to leave the door locked.

"I'm pinned against the apartment." Finn wasn't responding, but unless he had a cruiser driving down the street, I didn't need him to.

A thick Dur-Alf shield formed in the street and the ghostly shape approached, highlighting golden orange from the flames as they came into focus. A woman with dark clothing, hood, and a black veil slunk forward. She fired off a Mer lifting spell, though she held a gun ready at her side.

I had to burn a little energy for a second shield as the blue tip of the spell wormed at the edge of my first. When I fouled her spell, a thunderous blast from Dur-Alf crashed directly on my shields, trying to wear them down. It had flown in from the left of her, giving me a direction for another witch.

A ghostly hint of a second witch moved at my side, closer to the corner of the house.

The woman glanced at Leah, prone on the road. I inhaled sharply. What would I do if they threatened to shoot her in front of me? It would come to that if I let it.

"I'm pushing forward."

"Kristen?"

Shoving both of my shields through the debris of the hedges, I sent one toward the approaching witch to my left, a man from the shape of his frame. The second, I pushed toward the direction where the blasting spell had come from.

This appeared to leave me open to the woman as I raced down the sidewalk toward her and Leah with my weapon aimed. As I hoped, she slid to the edge of the shield. Since each of the witches were able to maintain barely one spell at a time, they didn't expect more than a couple from me.

I lobbed my blasting spell just past her, targeting the air one pace behind.

As she fired, I had a third shield up. Her bullet sunk into Dur-Alf thickened air two feet from my face. Firelight gleamed off the metal.

She tried to dodge my blast but stepped back into the target area instead. I winced when her black clothing shredded. I didn't have time to worry about her, though.

Through Haven, I could see residents peeking out windows of the apartments I'd just moved from. I needed some sirens behind me soon.

"One down."

I fired a blind gunshot toward the corner and dashed deeper into the street. An apartment door opened across the way — and quickly closed.

Exhausted, I dropped all shields and built a new one at my left side as I ran toward Leah and the SUV she'd nearly reached. She was protected somewhat from the more distant witch, but exposed to the one at the corner of the building.

My feint drew the attacks to me. Two binding spells splashed off the back edge of my shield before I was three steps into my run.

"I can't get to Leah." They would shred her with bullets or blasting spells if I got too close without heavy shielding that I might not be able to maintain.

Spinning behind my shield, I took aim and fired at the Haven ghost of a man now exposed beside the apartments. The acrid scent of spent gunpowder wafted around me, and the shot rang in my ear. I cringed when he cried out and dropped. If my shot was true, I'd hit center mass, but worrying about killing one or two witches wouldn't protect Leah.

The woman who I'd shredded with a Dur-Alf blast hadn't moved from where she lay. "Two down."

Dragging my shield between me and the Nissan SUV, I raced for the sidewalk across the parking lot. A bullet from my left gutted the windshield while two more thudded into metal. Steam hissed from the engine as I circled around the front to the sidewalk.

He was moving closer, and the third man was clear in Haven now. He wound through parked cars farther up the street. We had danced on opposite sides of the Pathfinder until I stepped to the front. Now, he crouched against a small sedan for cover as he fired into my shield. Sirens broke through my focus as they wound through the development.

"I've got backup coming." They might be more distracting than helpful.

With my shield thick in front of me, I aimed at the man, forcing him to drop behind the car. He lobbed a blasting spell over the top of the vehicle, and I shifted my shield in time. At least he wasn't focused on Leah.

The hood and grill of the Pathfinder shredded in plastic shards, and metal crumpled and groaned. Even as my shield weakened, I risked a blasting spell out of Dur-Alf and tossed it to the front of the sedan the man hid behind.

"Kristen?"

"I'm okay."

I didn't pull a shield next, but a binding spell, which I held ready as I dashed down the side of the ruined Nissan. Energy low and legs tired, I couldn't move as quickly as I wanted.

Leah's form was ahead, trapped on the asphalt. The

unmoving shape of the woman rested to my left in the middle of the street, and the dwindling light of the man I'd shot was across the parking lot by the flaming building. He was dying. The entire right top of the apartments was alight, and fire had burst through windows.

My focus was on the witch to the right scurrying away in a crouch from my slow moving blasting spell. He'd erected a shield, wisely, but wasn't tracking my mad race to get behind him.

I timed the throw of the binding spell perfectly, so it circled wide behind him. My dash gave me a clear view of him as I reached the middle of the street. With only the slightest adjustment, it snapped about him and dropped him face first. My blasting spell took out the windshield of the sedan, but barely blasted sand in his face from the distance he'd gained.

I staggered to a panting stop in the middle of the road and spun slowly. "Three down. I hope that's all they got." My legs wanted to give out as I sidled toward Leah. "They're going to need fire and ambulance."

Weapon still drawn, I knelt beside Leah and tore the Dur-Alf binding off her.

She sprung up with a growling curse. "Crap."

Holstering my weapon, I remained kneeling. The odor of burning plastic hung in the smoke beginning to thicken the air. Leah moved toward the woman on the asphalt. "Wait. Let me bind her." Non-witches couldn't tell whether I'd bound someone or not.

Leah paused. Her jaw was tight. Being bound and exposed usually brought angry responses and fear.

I didn't have time to rest with the local enforcement coming. We needed to control the scene. Wincing from the wounds in my leg, I pushed up, drew a spell from Dur-Alf, and bound the woman. "One more over here." The spell from Haven was fading, and his had dwindled to a near hint.

Leah pulled out her phone and began to take pictures for Tomas. "Thanks, Kristen. God, that sucked."

I headed for the man I'd killed. My lips tightened. I could never fully justify someone dying by my hand, but when I fired, I aimed for center mass. Law enforcement officers who didn't wouldn't often survive.

A well-groomed ornamental shrub and tree had been his cover. The sedan a few feet away would have been a better choice. He wore a black neck gaiter, as the woman had. His dead eyes stared at the smoke billowing from the building. At his sternum, his black turtleneck shirt glistened wet.

As I took his picture, I recognized him. "One confirmed dead. Manny."

For the first time in a while, Tomas spoke over the comms. "I didn't track any movement, so he didn't bring his phone."

I sent him the picture anyway. Two shapes scurried across the grass behind the burning house, causing me to flinch. Residents with their arms full and a cat carrier dangling from one hand escaped away from us, skirting a pond in the back. Eventually, the community would determine the gunfight was over and come to yell about it.

The siren growing louder came from one vehicle. I sighed and turned toward our last witch, bound, alive, and awake. Leah strode faster across the asphalt and had already reached him. "Finn, what's the ETA for fire and rescue?"

"You should have a crowd in the next five minutes. I've told them to check in with Leah before they approach. David and Pyre are twenty minutes out."

This had been a trap, another ruse that would point

firmly to Iliodor for most of my team. Lambert was behind this. He might be working for Iliodor, or just trying to please him, but I had no doubt who was pulling the strings and who had killed Bea. Where was he taking Clara?

Blue lights flashed on the buildings and the ruined Nissan from a squad car racing toward us. "Thanks. Apologize to the agent about his bucar."

"That bad?"

"Yeah," I replied, cringing at the buckled hood. Leah's flash lit the face of the man I'd bound. My eyebrows raised at the uncovered and recognizable long face. "We found Oscar Rainer."

TWENTY-THREE

I rolled kinks out of my shoulder as Leah turned toward the arriving squad car. "Well, I should start checking our guests while you deal with them." Nodding toward the officers, I knelt beside Oscar.

"I hate dealing with locals. Men especially." She sighed and trotted past the Pathfinder and the bound, unconscious witch.

Oscar's long face stared at the night sky and smoke above. I'd leave him fully bound until Marie arrived. "Well, what do you have in your pockets?" Under his sweater, he wore a white T-shirt that stunk badly and needed a good wash. His black cargoes were fresher and contained a phone. "I've got a phone. Locked. Want an emergency call, Tomas?"

Tomas swore. "Unless you want me to sift through fifty phones in the neighborhood." Shaking my head, I hit the emergency call on the locked phone, put it on speaker, and continued rifling through too many pockets. Oscar had keys and a fob. I pointed it around me, clicking, but no car unlocked. "He's got keys and a car fob. Toyota." He also had a black earbud.

Leah was describing a fake scenario to the officers where the area needed to be locked down against unexplained contamination, but the fire department would be clear to set up once they arrived.

"911, what's your emergency?"

I rattled off the address and described the inferno lighting up the clouds behind me — that they already knew about. He was kind enough to thank me anyway. Tomas could take pointers from the dispatcher. I tucked the belongings I'd found into my pocket when I stood.

As I ambled toward the woman, Leah leaned against the cruiser's hood, talking to one of the officers while the other flashed lights inside windows and waved residents back. A second car was pulling up already.

My first victim was awake. Blinking was part of the autonomous system that remained active along with breathing, heartbeat, etc. I cringed as I noticed my blast had scraped clothes and flesh from her shoulder and neck. Pain receptors also remained active. "Finn, do we have someone medical coming in to take care of the survivors?" I couldn't release a witch to regular EMTs without risking their lives, and they'd misdiagnose the binding.

Finn didn't get to reply.

"Leah, Kristen, what do you got over there?" Marie spoke over the comms as I rifled through the woman's empty pockets.

"Oscar is awake. Manny's dead. The woman is alive, but injured and needs medical. I've got keys to a possible car and Oscar's cell." I checked her ear and pulled out an earbud. "They had comms."

"Amelia Agnos. I've sent her file to your emails." Tomas seemed like he corrected my anonymous woman statement, rather than mentioning her name for the first time. I held a breath, recognizing my reaction to him.

"Firebomb?" Marie asked.

Leah answered, walking toward me. "We're fine, Pyre. Neighbors are evacuating, and I've cleared the police to cordon off the area and focus on the building." The street and buildings were lit with bizarre shadows, red and blue lights, and firelight. She reached me and gestured toward Amelia's legs and toward Oscar. "We'll try to get them off to one side to keep out of the way of the firefighters."

I frowned but grabbed an ankle, and we dragged the poor witch across the asphalt to the other side of the steaming Nissan. For all the death and torture Lambert had inflicted on people, I still didn't need the woman to suffer over it.

"We'll be there in a few minutes. Do we have Oscar's car?"

"Not close enough for the fob to react," I answered.

"Keep looking."

We left Amelia beside Oscar, and I followed Leah to Manny's body. In any other scenario, with any other official agency, the body would not be moved unless it directly restricted fire trucks. When we finished dragging his body to Oscar and Amelia, I opened the back of the bucar and sat on the edge. Whatever energy I'd gained from the quick snack, I'd spent.

Leah dug through Manny's pockets, saving me the task. This had all been another trap meant to distract us. It had worked. Lambert and Clara were long gone. We had been closest to them when we'd stormed the barn an hour or so ago. If he was as sharp as I expected him to be, they'd be almost a hundred miles away and moving fast.

"You look like crap." Leah stretched up to hold the top of the hatch. "Let me grab your stuff from the front."

"Thanks." The horns of a firetruck sounded in the development, getting nearer. The police had moved closer and around us. One had gotten keys from a resident and moved the mini SUV out from the front.

I straightened as she dropped my stuff beside me and wedged hers beside it. "Finn," she asked over the comms, "where's the closest place to park that's not in this development without having to come through the gate?"

"Neighborhood northeast of you."

Leah spun and pointed toward the front of the Pathfinder. "That's where they came from." She held out her hand for the fob. "I feel the urge to keep moving."

She had been stuck staring at the road during the fighting. I squeezed the fob out and handed it to her. "Have fun."

My hunger surged once I ate the tiny package of cheese, crackers, and almonds. I was through my bag of goodies from the gas station by the time Leah spoke on the comms. "Sending you a plate, make, and model, Tomas. It's not a rental that I can tell. Clean as a whistle."

"Finn?" Marie asked over the comms.

"I'll get the local FBI to tow it, Pyre." He coughed. "I can't say they're enjoying cooperating with us. I've got resources coming in to help lock down the site off of Speedway International, but they're going to have to hold it for six more hours."

A horn honked in the background of the comms, and I assumed it was for Marie's driving. The police were scurrying to wrangle people and their own cars out of the way as the firefighters trundled down the road with lights flashing.

Tomas piped over the comms with an excited tone. "Pyre, Oscar received a call from an active burner twenty minutes ago. Just the one time. They're stationary about half an hour from the site of the fire."

I straightened at the potential lead. It might or might not be Lambert, or perhaps another witch or coven involved in the kidnapping plan. Why else would you call at four in the morning?

"Leah, Kristen, I'm—" Marie paused while David spoke in the background, muted "—four minutes out. Be ready to go. I'm taking both of you. If we've got Lambert or Iliodor, it won't be easy. We'll interview Oscar and Amelia later. Finn, make sure the local officers stay clear of the bodies until local FBI can man the site."

"I did hint they might be contaminated," said Leah.

"Good. Hopefully they lean toward radiation rather than Ebola."

My mind foggy from exhaustion, I found the fire-fighters and emergency people distracting as they prepped to deal with the fire. There was a pause over the comms, so I asked my question. "David okay?"

Marie scoffed. "Slurping. I have him off comms for now." He mumbled something in the background. "Stow it, David."

Smoke hung over us and hazed the lights. I shoved the last half of a protein bar in my mouth and piled everything including my purse into my go bag. We'd be lucky if Marie slowed down to pick us up. Before Tomas could find new things to chastise me over, I dug out my phone and searched for his emails.

Still drained, I squinted to focus on the map he sent of the property nestled in woods that appeared mostly pine. There were only a couple neighbors including a reptile center, which I assumed had alligators.

A man named Victor Barnes owned the DeLand property and had arcane ties but no direct links to Oscar, Lambert, or Iliodor. An older man, I found it odd that he suddenly joined this group. His phone was active at the residence, but there was no clue he'd ever contacted anyone connected to the kidnapping. The burner that Oscar had called prior to the attack outside the burning house remained on at the location as well. Tomas had left notes on internet usage and known associates as pending, so I knew he was digging deeper.

The apartment hissed as water finally sprayed onto the flames. The inferno had spread to the entire building.

"Coming up the road behind the firetrucks; where are you?" Marie's voice had the sharp edge of impatience that had me and Leah hop with our bags in hand.

We jogged across the road, catching the attention of the local officers. Leah veered off to speak with a red-haired woman. I hesitated then ambled toward the barricades searching for Marie and David.

The FBI had loaned them a two-door Honda Civic with a driver's door that had been damaged and pounded back into shape. Faded black paint lit an ominous dull red under the emergency lights.

Moving slower than usual, David creaked open his door and stood beside it, sucking on the red straw of a "juice" pouch. Marie peered through the windshield impatiently.

I grimaced mockingly as I slid past David, tossed my go bag into the back, and squeezed in after it. "Nice ride." It smelled like weed inside.

"Stow it." Marie rubbed a hand over her smooth scalp. "What's your thoughts on this lead?"

Go bag tucked on my knees, I searched for the seatbelt. "If I were Lambert, I wouldn't be anywhere near here. I'd be a hundred miles in any direction."

"Finn made that harder than you might think with his roadblocks. What do you have, Finn?"

"Tomas has a couple models running, but the odds are in the high nineties that they did not get past my blocks on Speedway, I-95, or I-4 before I had them under control. That left plenty of back roads, mostly dirt, but I have four helicopters searching now, and local enforcement monitoring exits on those. That includes a power line road.

"There are two developed areas they could have reached, which we've blocked exits from. Oscar received a call from within the one closer to DeLand."

I hadn't realized how efficient Finn's cordon had been. "Well, then we have a chance before he tortures Clara. Excellent." My seatbelt locked into place as Leah grunted, wedging into the seat beside me. "I'd say we need to keep vigilant. We've fallen for a number of misdirects already."

Marie snorted. "Agreed."

The Honda groaned under the weight of all of us when David climbed back in. Leah and I fit in the back seat, where Finn would have scraped his dreads against the ceiling. Our own body odor and spent gunpowder battled the sweeter scent of weed as the passenger door closed.

Circling close to the barricade, Marie turned the car around while David brought up directions on his phone. I considered taking a nap if the ride would take us half an hour, then Marie swerved around a nosy resident walking their dog in the street to ogle at the fire.

"Should we wait for the other team to arrive?" I watched the mirror, waiting for Marie's eyes to lift and catch mine.

"We can't risk them getting anything from Clara," she said.

Hoping and dreading that Lambert might be at the property, I pulled up my phone to see how the four of us alone might get Clara out safely. He'd outplayed us each time. If Lambert were waiting for us at the property, he'd be prepared for an incursion with traps and other technology. He didn't rely just on magic. In a normal breach, SWAT would knock out the power but lose the advantage of surprise. "I have an idea."

TWENTY-FOUR

"First, Finn, we're going to need a utility truck from the local power company." Before he could ask, I started explaining. "Assuming this place is as well protected as the other locations, there will be cameras to monitor the outside and radios to keep track of local police." I picked at my curls, frowning. "If we start working with local police right now, we can send a message that the FBI is beginning a sweep, far from this residence. If Lambert bites on that, he'll assume we're focused there. Then we blink the power on and off."

Finn spoke over the comms. "Recycle their cameras?"

"More to warm them up to a black-out. Use the police again to announce an accident on the main road. Hazardous wire situation. I wouldn't be surprised if Lambert doesn't have more eyes and ears than we know. Driving in this clown car might set off an alarm. My thought is to get as close to him as possible, then lull him into expecting his power to go out. It takes one card out of his deck. He still might have the grounds wired to blow and wards plastering the walls, but he relies on technology as well."

There was a long enough silence from Marie that my stomach knotted. She finally spoke with a slow exhalation. "How long, Finn?"

"I've got a call out now to get us the utility truck, might have to widen that and get you any kind of company utility van. Should be cover enough. Tomas will handle the power cut off. I've already set the ball rolling on that. It's going to add an extra half an hour at least."

Marie swore under her breath. "Set me up a location to connect to the utility vehicle."

David lifted his lips off his straw. "Shotgun."

"Stow it."

An hour later, I shifted uncomfortably on the floor of the van as we raced down the tiny road that I hardly believed could accommodate an oncoming car. Pine trees made for a tight wall on either side. Marie showed no intention of slowing, though we were close to the property.

Tomas had flicked the light as we passed the reptile center, and floodlights were just coming back on at the house to our right. If I guessed our location from the map, Leah and I would be dropped off before the next property's driveway. Marie and Finn wanted us to split into two teams to meet at the west side of the house. I thought it was too dangerous.

We all agreed on getting as close as we could before trying to draw them out. Unlike most hostage situations, we weren't concerned about them harming Clara until they were down to their last stand. They'd already disposed of Bea, but they needed the older witch.

Marie decelerated quickly, and I rocked away from the back door. "Ready?" she asked.

I really hoped she planned on stopping.

Leah opened the door and hopped out without hesitating. You'd expect a werewolf to jump out of a moving vehicle.

Shifting, I stuck my legs out, willing to risk it, but Marie tugged to a stop. I closed the door quickly but quietly. She accelerated slowly, rumbling past the driveway and mailbox.

The main house sat over two hundred feet back from the entrance to the driveway, just beyond a silver sedan, and pine trees grew tight around the drive with only a glimpse of a lawn by the house. At the back, to the right of the house, sat a large three-car garage where we guessed they hid the trucks.

"Local FBI moving into place, Pyre." Finn sounded as tired as I felt. While we'd been waiting for a pair of grumpy guys to drop off the van, Finn had been tightening the noose around our planned target. I hated wondering if this were just another distraction.

Leah and I would approach from the northwest side while David and Marie drove due south and cut through the woods, hoping for no wards there. We all wished Finn were with us. Two witches were better than one in this case.

The eastern horizon was lightening, but with clouds and dense trees, a thick blanket of darkness hid everything under the brush. Without daylight, I had to follow Leah as she navigated with better eyesight. Down the drive, the buildings were dark shadows.

The rumbling of the van dwindled as birds were making their morning calls. David spoke over the comms. "Everybody hear me okay?"

"Yeah," I said. "How you feel?"

"Sick. Poisoned. Defiled. Violated."

"I feel like this conversation is toxic."

He grunted. "Be careful. Finn, we just turned off the main road."

"Thanks, David. I'll lock it up."

The locals had been instructed to put down chains and keep back. We had to hope they weren't exposed to magic, at least to the level they couldn't dismiss it.

Our split team was to meet at the garage if we weren't interrupted. We all assumed Leah and I would pick up some heat first, being closer to the entrance.

We could hear the van turn off and the doors softly close over the comms. "Move it."

Leah sighed and stepped off the road. As she stepped into leaves, my chest tightened. Despite fatigue, my senses sharpened as we committed to move forward. My job was to tug at the realms and make sure we weren't about to walk into a ward. After the traps set for us at Clara's house and the apartment complex, though, we were just as likely to trigger an IED.

"Power down throughout neighborhood. Monitoring cell traffic." Tomas sounded satisfied over the comms.

As before, I wouldn't use Haven until we had no other choice, but I tugged lightly at Mer and Dur-Alf so I could spot a ward within twenty feet or so. It would light up for any witch watching who was within that distance, but they'd also see the shield I maintained a pace ahead of Leah if they were that close.

The birds quieted as we neared, but those further from us were in their morning glory as they awaited the sun. Leah stopped, sniffing the air, and I froze mid-step. "We've got them, Pyre. I recognize a couple of the scents, matching those who were in the other house. Fresh." Slowly, she continued her step.

The attached garage was on the right end of the house,

while dark windows marked the rest, most of which were under an overhang near the front door. Plants and wicker furniture made the building appear almost homey. I braced against the rising pressure in my chest and continued to scan the area over Leah's left shoulder.

I could make out the shape of the separate garage behind the house, where the pale drive stretched. Marie and David would be coming out of the woods just to the right of it.

Dur-Alf lit brightly at the end of the garage as someone launched a blasting spell in our direction. Their aim was sloppy and off target, so I swiveled our main shield slightly to the left and pulled a second one to overlap it at our sides.

Leah jerked with a cough and paused. It took me until the gunshot echoed to realize she'd been shot. "Leah!" Gasping, I threw another shield in front of her. The ill-aimed blasting spell, a ruse to get me to leave her unpro-tected, startled me as it tore into the brush harmlessly.

Ya Keya misted around us as she staggered into my arms, breath wet and thick, then slid to the ground. I hadn't seen the muzzle flash, so I pulled all three shields tighter around us and whipped a blasting spell to the front corner of the attached garage.

"Leah's hit." My hand twitched as I felt wet blood through her Kevlar. My finger found the puckered edge. "High caliber. Through the vest." It would be a poisonous round.

Haven bloomed around me, tossed from the other end of the building. We lit up brightly along with a figure crouched behind a shield where my blast had gone off and another approaching behind a shield from the other end of the house. Three, maybe four lighter ghostly shapes milled inside the house.

Gurgling blood bubbled from Leah's mouth. She could change and heal quicker, but she wasn't.

"We need to get the bullet out, don't we?" Leah wouldn't be able to answer me.

The sniper's gunshot cracked again, and a long round nearly made it to my face. I swapped the shield for a fresh one and drew a pointed lifting spell out of Mer. I doubted Leah could ignore pain like David did. "Sorry. This is going to hurt."

A blasting spell crashed against my shields, and I swapped out the weakest while I pushed Mer into Leah's chest. She tried to scream as I dug for the bullet. This wasn't heavy muscle like David's leg; past the ribs were soft lungs. I had to dig deep before I touched it. The toxic metal burned at my spell, but I dug away at it, getting a grip. "Almost there."

Marie growled, and I refocused enough to see her tail dragging a man through a torn garage door at the building in the back and a glimpse of a rifle flung from his hand.

The man at the end of the attached garage had turned to fire at David and Marie, and I momentarily lost one of my shields when I whipped a beelined blasting spell for his exposed right shoulder. David, who had been racing forward, jumped back from the explosion.

I moved the bullet to the edge of Leah's vest and grabbed the blood-drenched toxic round with my fingers. "Got it."

The man approaching from the far corner was close enough for me to recognize as he began tapping rounds into my shields. Logan Curley belonged to Lambert's coven.

I replaced one shield, sagging against Leah. "Come on, shift."

I didn't hear her breathe, gurgling or otherwise.

Healing with Earth barely worked well on me, and I really shouldn't have tried it on a werewolf, but I wasn't about to let her die. Pulling what reserves I had, I pressed the muddy Earth realm against her chest and into the wound.

The mist of Ya Keya seemed to buzz, and the Earth spell thickened in resistance.

"Leah?"

The surrounding woods exploded with three blasting spells as two more witches exited the house and began tossing magic.

My hands trembled, forcing the healing Earth realm into her chest and refreshing a weakened shield.

Marie and David were in a firefight beside the back building.

So far, only one of the witches was down. I'd targeted him directly with a blasting spell. He might be dead. The three in front of the house were readying more blasting spells; they could see my shields were weakened and ratty.

"Leah?" I was close to giving up. She wasn't breathing, shifting, or giving me any sign of life. I'd poured all my energy reserves into the spell, and I'd failed.

A trio of blasts rocked under my shields, driving dirt and leaves into the bubble I'd created. I couldn't see David and Marie through the debris.

Leah coughed and gagged, her eyes opening large and wild before her skin rippled with shifting muscle. "Crap," she growled.

I laughed, nearly blacking out. Replacing one shield, I let Leah and Ya Keya roll away from me. Her facial muscles rolled into a wolfish form, then back, but her eyes were tired, still close to fading.

The three were readying another volley, so I dropped my tattered shields, clamped one over Leah's prone body like I had done for David earlier, and stumbled to my feet to stagger toward David and Marie. I needed to draw the fire away from Leah while she regained her strength. "Leah needs help," I said to the comms, unsure who I was actually directing the comment to.

David grunted, and I watched him stiffen under a binding spell. I couldn't see who they fought behind the house.

Dropping to my knees as Logan Curley and the other two witches threw their blasting spells at me, I pulled a weak shield over my left side and a pinched out another spell. Before the Dur-Alf explosions tumbled me over, I spun the binding in a lazy arc, appearing to be aimed at Logan.

The combined impact of their blast rolled me three times as it ate through my shield. My ears rang, and my hair prickled with pine needles and leaves, but my binding spell slid far wide of Logan Curley's attempted shield. The woman closest to the front door, Jen Dawson from the short black hair, went down stiffly.

My vision tilted as I stood and marched toward David, pinned fifty feet away on the concrete drive. "Finn, Leah took a bad hit to the lung."

Marie's tail flashed toward the back of the house.

The distance to David was too far to cross without giving Logan and the witches an opportunity to attack. I'd already moved away from Leah to draw the attention from her. Hopefully, her shifting would heal her enough so she could join us. She didn't speak over the comms, and that concerned me.

On the lawn in front of the house, Logan had moved to release his bound cohort. I pulled my weapon and fired to distract him. They would regroup, and I was caught in the open, dragging my ass down the driveway with barely enough energy to create another shield. "Heading for David." I spoke for Finn and Marie, but didn't have the time to focus on her.

Beyond unlocking and lifting, I sucked at using the Mer realm. One in particular made me nauseous, but I didn't see a choice. Twisting a knot out of the realm, I used the Mer speed spell.

Time and space distorted as I focused my march toward David.

Speed was the wrong word for a spell that sent you skimming like a rock through time and space. David's vampire speed gave him similar effects, from what I understood.

Pizza had turned to bile splashing at the back of my throat as each stride moved me too far and the world blurred. My stomach churned, and my feet threatened to trip rather than land squarely on the pavement.

In three steps, maybe twice that, I fell in front of David and promptly puked on the driveway. Hands shaking, I tugged at the back of his head, loosening the binding spell.

"Huh," he said. "That's a new one for me. Vomit splatter while bound." His voice was amused as he pulled me up firmly, hand under my armpit. "Let's get you somewhere safe. Safer."

"Leah." My voice sounded distant, and my vision blurred. Witches could faint from fatigue if they used too much energy on magic. I was close.

"Shot. I heard. Not fun. Don't suggest it." He was pulling me back toward Marie amid echoing gunshots that I couldn't pinpoint. The haze of Tarus flowing around him blended with the dim predawn light, and the whiff of death that clung to him merged with the sharper scent of spent gunpowder.

He fired his weapon even as he maneuvered me. I was holding my own Glock, barely. The world spun as we approached Marie. I slipped out of David's grasp like water through fingers and pressed my lips to concrete.

TWENTY-FIVE

I could taste salt on my lips as I licked sand off them. We needed a shield, but even as I touched Dur-Alf green with my fingertips, I couldn't tug at it.

"Clear in the back," Marie said beside me with a satisfied tone, though gunfire continued around me. "Leah?" she called with a tone of command that would have brought any of us to react. There was no response over the comms, and my heart tightened. She and David fired beside me.

A bullet thudded behind us, and I pushed a soft palm against the gritty driveway to rise. Trembling, I failed. Fever threatened my skin, and my pulse barely rose. I couldn't just lie there stinking of sweat and inhaling gun smoke.

David grunted and shifted beside me. "All good. Took it in the vest."

Hands grabbed my shoulder and rolled me to my back. Marie's face appeared over mine. "Please don't mention this in the report." When her hand pressed against my neck and chest, golden Salmhalla covered my vision.

The liquid realm flowed warm at the edge of my skin, but where Marie touched, electricity snapped into me like a million static shocks. I gritted my teeth and arched slightly. Beyond the film of gold, her face blurred, and for a moment she covered all my vision in dark greens and purples swirling on flat glossy patterns.

Her power raged through me.

When she let go, I sat up stiffly and nearly crashed into her. The blood of the man bleeding at the side of the garage from my blast was as pungent as our different scents and the whiffs of gunpowder. Sounds were crisp with birds calling from distant trees, a man groaning inside the back garage, and the whistle of the last bullet from Lambert's coven. My heart pumped heartily, and my eyes caught every movement of the three witches firing at David crouched beside me.

From where I sat, I threw a shield in front of us, a blast aimed beside the closest witch forty or so feet away, and a curving binding spell for Logan at the back of their group.

"What was *that*?" I asked Marie as I jumped up to a crouch. Energy raged inside me, and I imagined my hair standing on end three feet from my head.

"Nothing happened," Marie emphasized. "Get to the back. Stealth. We'll make noise out front. We need to secure Clara."

My blast threw Jen Dawson rolling out of sight behind the corner. She and Logan had both tried to bring out shields, and he'd nearly blocked my binding, but the blast had distracted him.

Strength surging, I wanted to stand toe to toe with these witches. However, Marie was right. We needed to sneak up on whoever held Clara. I didn't believe Lambert was a fair loser.

I wanted to ask him why he'd killed Bea.

We were far from the corners of the attached garage, so I tossed a Haven detection spell to my left, deep in the front yard, marking the three witches brightly. It faintly highlighted two ghostly shapes deep in the house and the man close to us by the side of the garage. I tossed a binding on him, turned and jogged toward the groaning man in the garage, and bound him as well.

Circling wide toward the rear building, I left David and Marie to deal with the last witch standing in the front yard. They parried gunshots with my shield still holding.

The sky was starting to lighten with the silhouettes of birds darting between trees. The backside of the house was deep in shadow. A screened-in porch stretched along all but the garage. Aluminum poles and screening were shredded from what I guessed had been Marie's tail. Five yards away, an unconscious man lay bleeding, near death.

"Moving in," I whispered. The energy Marie had somehow imparted on me left me aching to act, move, and speak. A smile flicked at the corners of my lips. She'd broken some rule to do it. Maybe Finn would talk about it.

A set of sliding French doors had been closed and carefully covered with thick curtains, while a smaller door stood ajar and revealed white walls. The two shapes were toward the front, where gunfire echoed. One appeared to be sitting. I needed that to be Clara. If I found her dead, crushed, I felt like I'd blast Lambert from the inside out. He had to be the figure standing.

I made out hints of a kitchen, then turned sharply. I hoped the people ahead of me faced the front; otherwise, Haven would light me up.

I slid through a top panel of the porch, where the screen flopped over a bar bent into a "v" shape. A glass table had been shattered, but the remains were far to my left. Plucking a binding spell in one hand and a shield in the other, I crept for the door.

There was a gap of eighteen or twenty inches that exposed the kitchen counter and wood floor, but not wide enough for my hips. I pushed my right shoulder and head inside.

Brick covered the kitchen, but otherwise bright white walls helped expose the shaggy brown-haired Lambert talking in the darkness, wearing the same dark outfit as his crew. He stood in front of the heavily draped front window. My Haven spell still lightly marked the others fighting outside. I flinched as he glanced to his left, where Marie and David were pinned behind my shield.

"Three and half minutes until reinforcements," Lambert said.

Perhaps he didn't know Finn had locked down the outer perimeter with local FBI. It would be worse if he did and still planned on their help.

Clara wore beige coveralls that highlighted the dusty green Dur-Alf that bound her. She'd been positioned in a chair at a dining table, facing a red metal canister sitting atop a green and white tablecloth.

I had no doubt there was an explosive inside the container. Was annihilation a last ditch threat, did he plan a suicidal end, or was he hoping to cover his escape with a fiery display? Anger flushed my cheeks. If I failed this rescue, he would kill us all.

Despite the gunshots outside, I could hear Lambert clearly from across both rooms. "They are coming in as EMTs, so the FBI won't have time to react until we've neutralized them." He chuckled, like he enjoyed the carnage swirling about him.

My tension loosened when Finn whispered over the comms, "Got it. I'll alert them."

Lambert's laugh grew louder. "We'll all just slip out of here once I blow this place."

I could only imagine he spoke to two witches still engaged on the front lawn. They would hardly be as amused dealing with David and Marie. At least I knew his plan for the explosive, not that he couldn't adjust once I moved on him.

He had to be slightly unhinged, and I needed to attack decisively. Still, I couldn't bring myself to shoot him without attempting a solution that left him alive.

Pushing an elbow against the door slowly, I managed a step onto the polished wood floor without alerting him. The back entrance aligned to the right edge of the kitchen, giving me a view of most of the dining room, but not all of it. Lambert, leaning to peer at Haven, shifted away from being a clear shot.

"Did the witch go to help the werewolf? Anyone have eyes on her?"

I smiled, lifting my binding spell in my left hand. I'd go with it first, if I could keep the element of surprise.

The floor creaked under my second step, and he spun to whip a blasting spell straight at the back door.

If I hadn't been holding a shield spell in my right hand, he might have shredded me. Instead, I had a moment to release it and divert the blast to the left of me. It ripped into the kitchen to tear off cabinet doors and rattle pans.

My step forward through the aftermath brought a snarl from Lambert. I had one chance to stop him from killing Clara and me, and I couldn't risk it all on a single binding spell.

"Why'd you kill Bea?" I asked, not because I expected an answer, but to gain a single moment of distraction.

Bringing both of my hands forward, I scooped out

three more Dur-Alf spells and sent them flying across the kitchen into the dining room.

Lambert could see them all. Anger flashed across his face, giving me precious moments. Eyes widening fanatically, he spoke with a finality that chilled my bones. "Now, we all lose."

I had not seen the detonator switch in his hand, but had suspected something like it was nearby. As he flicked a toggle, my first Dur-Alf shield flowed over Clara bound in her chair.

A red light flashed the first of two beats at the top of the bomb. During its slow pulse, my second shield slid between Clara and the canister, two feet from her face on the table.

My next shield was traveling to protect Lambert. Behind it, I snaked a binding spell, but the red light flashed a third time.

The blast hit him before my spell. Liquid fire, much like they used at the apartment, filled my vision and spilled around the edges of my first two shields. Flames roared across the ceiling and floor toward me. Only the broad second shield kept me from being engulfed. Lambert disappeared in the inferno, and the pressure of the blast deafened me.

The dining table flipped sideways, and Clara tumbled back toward the kitchen, tangled in the chair. My first shield around her was tattered and thin, but had protected her. Blazing walls billowed heat around me and singed errant hairs.

"Kristen?" Marie called over the comms.

I had no intention of losing Clara. They'd killed Bea. No more.

Lunging for the older witch, I wrapped us both in a new shield and dug at the Dur-Alf binding until she flinched and shook free. I prepped a larger shield and a blasting spell from Dur-Alf to try and douse some of the fire before we backed inside my spells to escape.

Clara blinked and scowled at the engulfed dining room. "Time to leave," she said.

When I shifted to stand, she grabbed my arm with her left hand. In her right, tufts of Ya Keya and Haven floated over her palm. They threaded into four knots in the air and pulsed to disperse into the space around us.

The heat disappeared and most of the light faded. In a hazy half-real world, I saw as if in a dream the charred table, an ashen tablecloth, and Lambert's smoking corpse. Ya Keya and Haven swirled about us.

"Hold onto my arm." Clara's voice sounded distant, but my ears were still ringing.

As we stood, I knew we were not completely in the Earth realm, nor Haven or Ya Keya, but on the blended borders of all three. "Did you tie the realms together?" I asked. Finn had worked two spells in tandem, but I'd never seen anyone weave them as Clara had.

"I did."

She stepped forward, through the burning table, toward Lambert's charred body. I felt no sympathy for the man; my only regret was not being able to question him. Part of me wanted to know why he killed Bea. Another part needed to know if Iliodor condoned this level of brutality.

The front windows had been blown out, as had the glass in the door. Flames ate at the tops of the frames, licking into the overhang and igniting the wicker furniture. Despite the smoke, I could see the last witch folding over as the pointed tip of Marie's tail slapped him to the side.

"I'm okay, Marie." We stepped through the half-wall below the window with a slight tug.

"Your comms won't be audible to her. I'll get us clear."

We stepped across the engulfed porch to the grass. Sprawled on the lawn, the witches were ghostly shadows in Haven, but a darker shadow also marked each core. As the last of the witches scattered on the lawn, Marie and David were jogging forward as if to risk the inferno. Where was Leah?

Clara strode far past the witches. "Is the area safe?"

"Yes." Safe enough. I needed to keep David from doing something foolish like trying to rescue me and to get help to Leah.

She twisted a hole in the haze surrounding us, and heat wafted off the burning porch. Firelight lit the grass and trees around us. Sounds popped into my ears.

". . . one of the witches escaped. Two down. Any sign of Kristen?" Finn asked.

Marie pivoted toward me and Clara with a raised eyebrow. "Yes."

David smiled. "Now that you mention it. She and Clara appear to be quite unharmed."

After tossing two binding spells on the unconscious witches, I gestured toward the woods at the front by the drive. "Leah. She needs help."

Clara turned to where I pointed. "Show me."

With the energy Marie had given me, I could heal Leah now. I forgot everything else and barged toward the front woods.

Marie's voice was insistent, but not sharp. "Lambert? Anyone else in the house?"

I cringed and glanced back, but didn't stop. "Incinerated himself. Building is empty otherwise." We'd survived, but it wouldn't feel real until I knew Leah was okay.

The sky had turned a lighter gray to the east, still not

showing any color from the rising sun. Clara strode with a calm assurance. There was no sign she was injured.

"Are you okay?" I asked.

She held my eye. "Thanks to you and your team. I appreciate it."

I thought of Bea and broke our gaze to focus on the woods where I'd left Leah. "They killed Bea." Clara likely knew.

"Lambert. I'm not sure what set him off, but he was raging at someone for failing. I didn't get the details. Bea said something, and he crushed her. I begged him to stop, but he wouldn't." Clara's lips tightened. "I don't even know why he took her. Killed my cats for no reason."

Leah appeared as a mound ahead, still protected under my shield. "Did he say what he was going to do with you?"

"A gift for Iliodor. Lambert was disturbed and not very coherent at times." She spoke so coldly about it all, that I chilled. "I did not get the feeling I was anything more than an item on Iliodor's wish list."

"Are you sure?" Marie asked over the comms. She and David were pulling Logan, closest to the fire, away from the burning building.

"Said as much." Clara lips twitched, as if she might have more to say. "His chimes knocked out Ya Keya and Dur-Alf. At least I couldn't touch them. He laid binding spells on me and Bea easily enough, and bragged about our capture when they carried us to the ATV."

"Chimes?" asked Marie.

"Best I can describe them. Some artifact that rang and knocked out most of my magic. I'd love to study it, if you find it."

Leah rested in the leaves on her side, as if sleeping. Even a few steps away, I could tell she was breathing regularly. Kneeling down, I tugged off the Dur-Alf shield. She had a musky scent beyond the blood, but appeared fully human again.

Clara wove Earth and Haven together, much like she'd done with Ya Keya earlier. This combination formed a thick fog that poured over Leah.

I'd seen what she'd done, but didn't know if I could replicate it. "What is that?"

"A very old healing wisp, taught to my mentor by the dragons. Try it. Leah is stable and will be quite healthy when she wakes."

I started tugging at Haven and Earth as she had, but the weave separated.

Clara nodded. "Keep trying. You've got it." Her eyes unfocused toward the east. "Marie, if I'd known what he was going to bring against us, and what he'd do, I would have killed them all in the first stroke. Screw the Consociation's prohibitions."

Her cold demeanor was lifting, and I saw it now as a lid on a simmering pot. Clara was angry. She had a right to be. So did I.

TWENTY-SIX

I managed blending Earth and Haven a few minutes later, and the sensations that vibrated through the spell were far different from using just the mud. Leah's body and consciousness seemed to travel back up the magic, helping me focus it where needed. A lot came through the connection. "I can sense Ya Keya."

"The infection, the effect, is at a cellular level, so it is easily recognizable. The same can be said with vampirism, though you would have a very difficult time healing a vampire beyond a simple tear."

I waited for a comment from David, but he said nothing. Finn and Marie had been heavy on the comms dealing with the aftermath of Lambert's cohorts attempting to break through the FBI cordon. Before the entire forest went up in flames, Finn had to get emergency vehicles to the residence.

It was another minute or two of healing before I knew Leah was rousing, before she opened her eyes. She glanced from me to Clara. "Ominous. I'd bet from the tingling that you two are up to something. I certainly feel a hell of a lot better."

"I'm glad." Clara smiled and let her spell fade, and I followed suit. She offered a hand to Leah, who took it but stood mostly on her own.

The horns and sirens of heavy emergency vehicles sounded in the predawn.

"Leah?" Marie asked.

"I'm good, Pyre. I need some protein and a solid day's sleep, that's all. I see Clara's good. Lambert?"

Marie didn't answer the question directly. "We've got a lot to wrap up. Finn has some Consociation teams almost here to help detain Lambert's people and some from a coven in Texas."

I frowned, imagining Lambert's crisp, burnt corpse. He'd brought it on himself. Shaking my head slowly, I signaled to Leah that the witch who'd caused all this hadn't made it. I'd go into details later.

We still had bound witches stacked up at the first two sites. Finn and his Consociation resources would be busy. As I ambled down the drive, approaching Marie, she tossed a set of keys to Leah. "Take Kristen. Get some food for all of us."

David cleared his throat. "Maybe I should go grab my cooler. I'll be right back."

He led the way in a wide arc past the burning house while Marie and Clara watched flames from beside a group of bound witches. The horns and sirens grew louder, getting closer to the street in front of the house. The sun colored a cloud orange to our left, and the birds serenaded as we moved away from the fire.

David poked at the hole in Leah's vest. "That hurt, I'd bet."

"Like stepping in front of a train."

"Yeah, that does hurt." David grinned. "Think we get to go home now? I'm out of suits." He dug at the hole in his pant legs.

"You just want to avoid Mika."

His smile wavered. "Perhaps."

TWENTY-SEVEN

Four hours and a stack of gas station egg sandwiches later, I stood with my team and Clara awaiting Mika and their team. The heat had climbed with the rising sun, and the tarmac stunk of sharp petroleum. I'd taken time to pull out some of the splinters, but still felt itchy.

The jet was slightly larger than ours, with perhaps an extra window. As the door opened, the first person exiting had sea foam, blue-green hair blended with wisps of yellow rising in a loose quaff from their prominent forehead and flipped back over darker hair. Large glasses with wine-colored rims dominated the middle of their face and high cheekbones. A bright smile grew into a toothy grin. "David. You look so hot when you go punk goth." I assumed it was a reference to his torn clothes.

"Thank you *so* much, Mika." David made sure the insult to his fashion carried in his tone.

Mika hopped the last few steps and ran directly to David. If anyone, they were dressed in all black goth and even had a black FBI sweatshirt hoodie. Barely an inch higher than me, they were barrel-chested and squat, but short legs ate up the distance. They slammed into David with a hug that staggered him.

Behind them, a quiet crew of three piled out of the jet plane. A tall mustached man with light brown skin akin to my own had thick black hair waving to the jawline. A pale woman appeared frail behind him, but sharp black eyes marked every one of us in a single footstep. Her long brown hair was a sharp contrast to the pixie-cut redhead behind her.

Bowing to Marie with a wave and a leg stretched out in front of them, Mika wore a smirk. "Pyre. You called, and we answered, but I fear we have arrived too late."

"Stow it, Mika. I appreciate you pulling your team off your project. We got lucky and closed the case. It could have gone worse." Marie cocked her head. "Phistrel, you shaved your beard?" She addressed the mustached man, who I tried to imagine with a beard.

"Reluctantly. I was undercover." Phistrel's voice was deep and melodious.

"And whined over every gnarled hair," said the redhead. She stuck her hand out to me. "You must be Kristen. I'm Dagen." The dark mist of Ya Keya blossomed around the werewolf.

The slighter woman offered her hand as well. "Olivia." Tarus bloomed about her, and she must have seen my surprise. "I've always been small — and okay with it." The vampire nudged her chin toward David. "Unlike some of us."

Mika bowed slightly, nothing like the show for Marie. "Mika at your service." They studied my face with obvious intensity. "You must send Tomas for a spin." The Merfolk gripped my hands, letting the realm of Mer ripple about them.

I frowned. "Why? What do you mean?" My question to Tomas would not be so vague. When I glanced at my team, Marie just shrugged.

"Hmm. Ask Tomas what I mean." Mika slid past to give Clara a hug. "Long time, sister. I hear we're taking a road trip."

I shot Marie a questioning glance. When she said we'd meet Mika at the airport on our way out, and Clara had joined us on the drive to the airport, I'd assumed they'd be flying with us.

Mika had returned to David, draping themselves off his ruined suit. "I thought we'd at least get a night together. A few drinks."

David raised his cooler.

"Ew. No. Something with rum." Suddenly Mer rippled, and Mika was a long-legged blond woman in shorts and high heels, with cleavage pressing against a gray T-shirt with a bright logo. Leaning up to kiss David, their illusion shifted to a middle-aged, balding man with average everything.

Marie snorted, her eyes locked on the two attendants unloading luggage from the jet. "Some discretion, Mika."

"They're not watching, and you know it." The dowdy man pouted and patted David's bottom before resting a hand casually on the red-headed Dagen. An illusion faded the werewolf's hair to gray and aged the woman with wrinkles.

I was glancing about casually as Mika wandered through their group.

Clara's sharper features were rounded, and a pleasant maternal figure fit into a yellow print dress. Phistrel was the only one to remain unaltered, and he walked their luggage inside with the handlers.

Mika gave me a smile despite the frumpy man they

wore as an illusion. "I hope we get to actually work together. You're getting quite the reputation." They hugged me, blurring the air with the blue-green of Mer and their illusion. "Be careful, or they'll want to move you to a less fun position."

After their comment about Tomas, and now this vague warning, I didn't react except to smile and nod.

Mika turned to Marie last. "Get some rest. We've got this. We'll meet up with the Guardian as planned. There won't be any trouble."

Clara approached me in her illusion, but her eyes were still intense and sharp. "I wish we had met under better circumstances. There are some people — memories — we will likely always associate with each other." She put her hand over mine and clasped it tightly.

I imagined Bea, bouncing about with a smile and a laugh at Clara's house, then crushed to the floor and cold. My throat tightened, and I blinked. "Well, I'll try not to focus on that." The crack in my voice betrayed me, and Clara embraced me with a deep sigh.

"We live in a strange new world that's difficult to navigate, but I believe you might be doing the right thing." She gave me no time to respond as she disengaged and walked across the tarmac.

With the other DRC team heading into the small airport terminal in Daytona Beach, I felt the heat rising with the sun.

"If we're going to get a tan, could we go to the beach?" David had lathered his mushroom paste over his skin, but appeared uneasy in the sun. "Scenery is better."

"Stow it, David. Finn?"

"They're ready for you."

Marie headed to our left, where just past a fuel truck, our jet plane waited. Leah stretched as we strode toward the attendants at the open door. "One, two hours? Sleeping the entire way."

I'd long since gotten used to flying in the small plane, with the heart-dropping bumps, though I wasn't comfortable enough to nap. Leah crashed before takeoff, and Marie focused on email, so that left David and me to chat between social media or emails. I didn't have the energy to focus on anything in depth, so even my puns were cheesier than usual. By the time we landed in Atlanta, though, I'd made a decision.

After 1 p.m. Marie swerved up to the FBI gate security, who were still checking IDs since the attack on the office. "Everybody get some rest this afternoon. We'll deal with reports tomorrow. Plan on a couple of days off after that."

"I'm going to check on one thing at the office, then I'll head home. Promise." I watched the mirror, checking for Marie's subtle nod. It was time I had a conversation with Tomas.

Standing in the hallway outside his door, I fought the desire to back down from the conflict and just go home. Sharp sweat reeked from my torn clothes. My hair had frizzed and stuck out farther on the right. Makeup had been a quick powder and gloss. I wasn't here for a date. Skin flushed, I strode inside Tomas's office.

The window still needed new glass, but there was no other sign of the incident. The damaged monitors had been replaced, and data waited on each one that didn't have a program running. I pushed aside an urge to ask about anything he was working on.

My stomach churned at confronting him. The scent of hot electricity hung in the room. Tomas didn't swivel his chair toward me, leaving me to speak to his back draped with long curly brown hair.

"You're rude to me," I said. The words sounded childish the moment I uttered them.

He typed on his keyboard. "I'm rude to everyone, according to reports. Is this revelation important?"

"Well, worse with me. It's noticeable."

"You're no different from anyone else. Nothing special." He put too much emphasis on the last comment.

"What have I done to deserve it?"

His head flinched, as if he resisted facing me. "Nothing," he said in a more reserved tone, lowering his usual high pitch. As quickly, he tried to dismiss me with a hollow placating promise. "I'll try to be more conscious of your sensitive nature."

My cheeks flushed with anger. "Why? There has to be a reason."

He still wouldn't turn to face me. "You've done nothing. You're new and still learning, that's all."

I had wanted to believe that at first, but now it was an empty excuse. "Tell me why." My tone had hardened, and I was close to spinning his chair to face me. My frustration and determination rose with each excuse he offered and the deeper he denied his reaction to me.

Tomas continued to type without speaking. One of the screens flipped from a list of linked data to an image of an older woman smiling in a rose garden. With gray curled hair and wrinkled brown-skin, wearing a wide-brimmed hat and dirty white gloves, she could have been a cousin of my grandmother.

"My wife has been fighting cancer for three years. With Herta's help, she's survived this long. It will win, eventually."

I blinked, unsure if this was meant as another excuse for his behavior, but what was I supposed to say? "I'm sorry to hear." Maybe he expected me to relent out of sympathy. Lips twitching, I straightened and readied to press him for an answer.

The image changed. I might have thought it was one of my photos, except the woman had a wreath of yellow flowers in her hair and wore a tie-dye. The likeness silenced me.

"It is as if someone is playing a cruel joke on me," Tomas said quietly, "reminding me of a life from over fifty years ago and what I'm on the edge of losing. I can't see you without thinking of her. It's not your fault." He spoke the last comment as if reminding himself.

Mika had been serious when they'd said, "You must send Tomas for a spin." Who else knew? Finn? Definitely Herta, and possibly Marie.

"Are we related — your wife and I?"

His answer took a minute. "No." We paused in his room silently for even longer before he spoke again. "I'll try to be conscious of my tone with you. It hurts to be reminded. I can't promise my bitterness won't leak through, though."

The silence became awkward before I excused myself. "Thank you for showing me this. I'll keep it in mind — when I'm feeling sensitive."

I stepped into the hall. My eyes teared over Tomas's wife. He'd known he would outlive a human, but that didn't make it easier. Wanting to talk through it, I stepped in the office, searching for Finn. He wasn't there, and I didn't head upstairs.

Instead, I headed home for the promise of a shower and some Häagen-Dazs. I begged off time with Astrid in exchange for a lunch date in two days. "I've got paperwork tomorrow, but I think I've got Thursday off."

"We can hit the café at Stone Mountain you mentioned. Huskers."

Exhausted, I agreed and slunk into my apartment, considering a tub to soak some of the tougher splinters.

It wasn't until after the next day coordinating reports that I met with Finn and his husband Gary early at the team's haunt outside the DeKalb airport.

After a long explanation, I asked Finn, "Did you know? The resemblance?"

His dreads swung as he shook his head. "I've never met her. I researched her briefly when I joined the team, so I've seen her driver's license photo. Glasses and gray hair. Now that you mention it, I can see it, though."

Gary, pale but always smiling since Finn had moved to a desk job on the team, reached over for my hand. "It's better that you know. You can gently remind him to respect you, and you'll both have a better understanding of the situation." He raised his eyebrows at Finn. "It's so much easier when you know what's going on."

Finn winced. "It's case related. I can't."

Gary squeezed my hand. "Over fifty hours at the office. Barely a word, and I wasn't allowed to even bring the baked tofu for a snack."

"We had him pretty busy. It was hectic."

Releasing my hand, Gary stroked his graying goatee. "He can be useful."

We all straightened when David strode in waving and calling out to us before hunting down a server to discuss his wine options. Marie and Leah slipped past him and took seats at the table.

"I've got word that Mika and team are heading back tonight. Our ward has accepted a Guardian at her new property. We can hope this is over." Marie flicked a smile to Gary. "Don't ask."

"Wouldn't think of it." Gary leaned against Finn with a smile.

A Guardian? Something for me to research when I got back to the office. I also planned on digging into whatever Marie had done to me when she'd recharged my magical batteries. No grimoire that I'd read mentioned a dragon-shifter able to do that.

Leah tugged at her pink chiffon blouse with a smile. "Anyone else planning on a spa day after all that fun?"

I looked forward to a day off with Astrid. We'd promised to do more together, but the timing rarely worked out. "Lunch and a little shopping," I offered.

Finn snorted. "I've got to head in for a couple of hours, but then weeding a garden bed, evidently."

"Marigolds," Gary explained. "How about you? Marie?"

"Reading." She flipped a menu over, though we all knew it by heart.

Gary grinned. "A cheap romance?"

She snorted. "I prefer history, and I've just acquired a text of Kizurra."

David and the server approached, stifling our conversation. "Chill the Pinot five minutes, please."

The young man smiled and nodded agreeably. "Is everyone ready to order something to drink?"

"Loblolly Double IPA," Marie said, then nodded to me.

I sighed, "Same."

Finn coughed and Marie raised an eyebrow.

"Well, beer pressure."

TWENTY-EIGHT

The next day I relaxed with Astrid and ate waffles at a clean café near Stone Mountain and a mall that promised some art supplies in my future.

"You've never had waffles?" I asked. "How is that possible?"

Astrid attracted attention with her knobby six-foot height and blue and purple streaks in her short blond hair. When she shrugged and gestured with her hands, more heads turned. "Are there not foods you haven't eaten?"

"I suppose, but have you never seen a Waffle House and wonder what that word meant?" I'd yet to see a Georgia exit without a Waffle House, or a back highway without a Dollar General.

"They are very good. I have learned that." She smiled. "I'm sure there is new food for me to try still." Her plate was half-finished, but she'd tucked her napkin beside it.

My food was long gone, and I was ready to head to the mall. "You mentioned flying next week. Where are you headed?"

"St. Lucia. I wish to study their grass."

I chuckled. "Beach grass?"

"Yes."

I hardly saw any reason to ask why, since she tended to love nature. "That sounds fun."

"You could come with me."

"I've got a trip coming up to visit my daughter."

Astrid smiled broadly. "You have said. Very important." She stood abruptly. "I will return." With her lanky gait, she headed for the bathrooms.

I nodded to my strange friend and pulled out my cell to check social media. I'd posted one of my latest cards on an artist forum, and it had gained some excitement. Eyes around the room followed Astrid's ungainly pace through the tables.

One older man, two seats away, watched me over his coffee. His face, with his gray hair and light eyes, was slightly familiar, as if I'd seen him on a show or in a magazine. Smiling at me, he put his coffee down. With ease for his age, he slid out of his chair and walked toward me.

Without a word, he took Astrid's seat. "Hello, Kristen. I've been hoping to meet you." Gray — no, silver eyes with black slashes like I'd never seen before were sad and sympathetic despite the smile. A slight nose and prominent eyebrows tugged at my memory. The gray mustache crouched over his lips, spreading with his light smile.

I gasped, recognizing Iliodor across from me. When I dug into Dur-Alf, my spell turned to dust.

"Just a moment of your time. A sales pitch, if you would." His finger stroked one side of his mustache. "Your skill is amazing. The Consociation will not leave you in the DRC for long."

Relaxing, I glowered at him. "You had Bea killed."

"Of course not. There would be no use in that action. Lambert had always been a bit impulsive, but he had gotten results prior to this unfortunate mess. My apologies, since he did act to further my interests, even if I learned of it after he'd kidnapped Bea and Clara."

"You're still responsible."

"Enough to offer an apology for your friend." Iliodor sighed. "We have so little time. I imagine you have read some of my treatises?"

"Some." Curiosity rivaled my desire to capture him. Marie would be livid to know how close he was to me.

"What do you think of my arguments? Do you believe that the world would benefit from knowing about the realms that the Consociation conceals from them?"

"No." I tried to sound sure of myself.

"Why not?" he asked.

I should be considering how to trap him, not arguing policy with him. "There would be chaos. Witch trials. Werewolves and vampires would be hunted."

He nodded slowly. "And after that?"

"Isn't that enough?"

His eyes sparkled intensely. "And after that?"

"I don't know," I said with a surprised honesty. I had never considered that far.

Iliodor beamed. "Exactly. Consider it. We'll speak again someday."

At the end, I expected him to attempt to recruit me. "What did you want, to risk this?" I motioned to Astrid's seat.

His eyes drooped with a sadness. "Just a chat. I can't expect more than that." He turned his back on me and began to head for the door.

Dur-Alf again turned to dust at my fingertips. I stood. "I can't just let you leave."

Customers were frowning at my loud comment. As I

took a step forward, Ya Keya misted the air about Iliodor, and he disappeared into the realm.

A mug crashed to the floor as one woman lost her grip. Excited mutters filled the room. Many had seen him disappear into thin air. Some customers were already standing, as if to leave.

It took me too long to pull out my phone. I'd have to report this. There was a mess in the restaurant that the Consociation would have to clean up. Iliodor had exposed magic on purpose. Reluctantly, I began dialing Finn's number. I had hoped for just one quiet, relaxing day.

AFTERWORD

I'm thrilled you made it here to the end of episode 5!

A review is always helpful if you enjoyed this story.

Contact us at Inkd Pub if you'd like to join the ARC team or Beta readers. support@inkdpub.com

I always enjoy hearing from readers, so please don't be shy. This episode formed in my mind during a trip to a convention in Daytona Beach where I stalked the drive-in church on a Sunday.

Would you be interested in a free short from David's perspective? An incident in his past?

If you haven't read it already, you can download from BookFunnel a very quick read. It'll sign you up for a mailing list during the download, but it won't activate unless you confirm on the follow up email.

David's Journal #21 https://BookHip.com/FRQGMPM

Demon

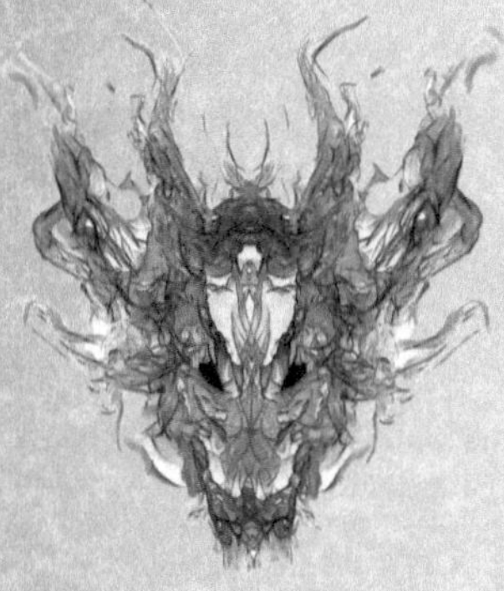

A demon is a rare inhabitant of the Tarus Realm who can be summoned to the Earth realm or cross of its own intent if given an opening. [1]

Their summoned forms often are a nightmarish mirror of their summoner with features designed to terrorize, such as claws, fangs, and horns. [1][2] Highly intelligent, they feed on strong emotions such as panic or rage. [2][3]

They are reported to rely on physical attributes for attack, but have been known to compel humans to act out their violence. [2][3]

(Cont. next page; Accounts of Demons in Tarus)

[1] Read Tinkanchtners's *The Art of Demonic Summoning*

[2] Read Kizurra's *Referene on Tarus Cryptids* Page 26 to 47

[2] Read Carey's *Of Demons and Jinns*

Dragon-shifter

The portion of a dragon exposed in the Earth realm which can mimic the aspect of a human.

Most of what is known about dragon-shifters has come from archaic grimoires with questionable translations. [1][2] There is at least one resident on Earth to coordinate with the Consociation. [3] Reportedly, a dragon-shifter is an exact replica of a human, unless they intend otherwise. [2][4] A witch would know on contact.

The details of their craft ability are shrouded in myth due to their self-expulsion from the Earth realm prior to the Akkadian wars was preceded by a slow withdrawal during the prior era. [1][2][4] They openly apologize for their interference with man, resulting in the rituals that brought about the vampires and werewolves. [3][5]

(Cont. next page; Role in Consociation)

[1] Read Yin's Volume IV of Realm Studies Pages 1340 to 1489

[2] Read Wooley's Anecdotal Studies of Salmhalla

[3] Read Ferno's Presentation of the Consociation

[4] Read Inhai Du Anya's Scriptures of the High Dragons Page 1-72

[5] Read Sover's On Madness

Draugr / Draughr

A common inhabitant of Tarus who can be summoned to the Earth realm, or cross of its own intent if given an opening.

Territorial they tend toward an unusual compunction to protect valuables.

Tall and strong they present as humanoid on Earth with no skin and sharp black nails. They possess reflexes and speed beyond humans.[1] Savage and instinctual on a physical level. Relatively low intelligence.

Magical or Arcane abilities: None

Note the Akkadian ritual listed in the 1911 appendix

[1]Read Macrin's Journal for an in-depth biological reference compilation of Merfolk research of the Draugr

Dwarf / Dwarves

Humanoid residents of Dur-Alf with a proclivity for exploration and research. Their earliest interactions with humans caused a wider disturbance than expected and their own sanctions for crossing to Earth were ignored by many of their more independant scholars and explorers. Brief conflicts existed between individuals as witches developed the ability to pass into the Dur-Alf realm.
Small in mass and stature, their biology is similar to Earth mammals. [1]

Conflicts erupted between humans and dwarves [2] as human witches and arcane users began to cross realms. Dwarves are especially biased against vampires.

(Cont. next page; Magical and Arcane usage)

[1] Read Macrin's Understanding Dwarven Physiology and Psyche

[2] Read Thant's War on Human Mutation

Kuru Kuru 

Mammallian bipedal residents of Dur-Alf though the only known description of their physical resemblance comes from two sources and both differ slightly. [1][2]

The Dwarves do acknowledge their presence and the Kuru Kuru have been given access to the Consociation. [3] They speak only to the Dragon delegation there and have some relationship with Dragons. [4]

Small in mass and stature, their biology is similar to Earth mammals with a flattened muzzle. Reports differ on fur (pictured), or with feathers. [1][2][3]

(Cont. next page; Magical suppositions)

[1] Read Kainin's Guide to Dur-Alf, Eden of the Realms

[2] Read Emily Randolp's Memoirs Among the Sprites

[3] Read Daesalu's Biography of Talat

[4] Read Ono Seyo's Conspiracy of the Consociation

Merfolk / Mer

   Mer, called Merfolk by the Consociation, have the ability to transform into similar mammalian shapes upon interrealm movement. [1]

   Little is known about their unaltered form except that it is a sea mammal of some type, hypothesized to be porpoise-like. [2]

   Their longstanding habitation of Earth's oceans ceased at the point when Earth witches and arcane users began using the Mer realm in magic which coincided with the interrealm movement of humans to Dur-Alf. [3] Merfolk returned to Earth during the formation of the Consociation at the urging of the dwarves with whom they had long enjoyed diplomacy and trade. [4]

   Many Mer research and work on Earth as part of their proposal to the Consociation for admittance. [5]

(Cont. next page; the impact of Merfolk on magical use by witches and the arcane)

[1] Read Sienna's Treatise on Earth's Devastation

[2] Read Tino Vangian Biography of Venis: Traitor of Mer

[3] Read Sienna's Treatise on Mer Isolation

[4] Read Tino Vangian Biography of Venis: Traitor of Mer

[5] Read Tino Vangian's Biograpy of Sienna

Revenant

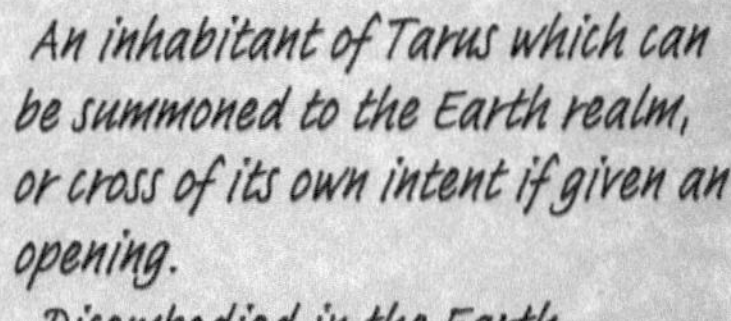

An inhabitant of Tarus which can be summoned to the Earth realm, or cross of its own intent if given an opening.

Disembodied in the Earth realm, they will seek to possess a humanoid corpse, or living entities with a weakened consciousness such as comotose or those near death.

Their corporeal control depends greatly on their prior experience. [1]

They range in intelligence and will avoid confrontation where possible.

Expellation is relatively simple depending on the skill of the witch. [2] Vampires have an innate ability to remove Revenants from their possessed hosts.

Magical or Arcane abilities: None

[1]Read Rasputin's Walks Among the Undead for a detailed observance of summoned Revenants

[2]See Appendix from 1892 - reference Possession

Vampire 

A vampire is a human-born crossover to the Tarus realm. They are infected with a Tarus symbiotic life form initially misunderstood as a form of magic inherited from Tarus. [1] The infection can be summoned, gained through prolonged contact with Tarus, or transferred by blood-to-blood transfer with a vampire. [2]

The human cells are mutated to a far more resilient state and can be controlled to an extent which allows the vampire to change facial features and extend their life. [1] [3] Strength and speed are are increased with minimal muscular and bone alterations. [4] Vampires are entirely resistant to infection, disease, and toxins. [3] Mental acuity does not change. Emotional reactions remain, though extended life spans have brought interesting results. [1] [3] [4] [5]

(Cont. next page; the Tarus symbiote)

[1] Read Tonsun's Illuminating the Mystery

[2] Read William Beckett's Becoming a Legend

[3] Read Annan's Study on Mutation

[4] Read Anonymous Confessions of Self-Hatred

[5] Read Macrin's Sapien Emotive Reponses Pages 21-88

Werewolf / Dreamer / Hunter

Born human they have developed a psychic and realm connection to Ya Keya. They are affected by their interactions and develop biological alterations. The connection can be summoned, by a ritual interaction with the bodily fluids of a mature werewolf, or through intense submersion in Ya Keya. [1] Longevity varies [2]

Transmuted form:
They gain 15–20% more mass directly from the Ya Keya realm. Reflexes, strength, and speed increase by 10–30% beyond their human norms. Eyesight and hearing are more acute though more age dependant than other attributes. [2]

(Cont. next page; loss of Magic and Arcane usage)

[1] Read Kizurra's History of Akkadian Werewolves - the Dawn

[2] Read Demot's Monograph for an in-depth biological reference

Dur-Alf

Visible indications are a dark-green color and a crumbling or dusty consistency.

Dur-Alf is a planet realm similar to Earth in that it orbits a singular star; it is the fourth of eight known bodies in the system and does not have any satellites. There are major land-locked bodies of water and large polar ice caps. [1] Rivers and lakes abound in most regions except near equatorial deserts. The seasons are mild, and wildlife is plentiful. [1] [2] The only known transplants from Earth are kestrels and a variety of water birds including swans, geese, ducks, and kingfishers. [1] [2] [3]

Humans are no longer welcome or tolerated in the Dur-Alf realm. [4]

Known bordering realms: Earth, Mer, Salmhalla, Mer, and Tique (described as a hostile realm [5]).

(Cont. next page; Known Species)

[1] Read Kainan's Guide to Dur-Alf; Eden of the Realms

[2] Read Emily Randalp's Memoirs Among the Sprites

[3] Read Yin's Volume VI of Realm Studies Pages 1289 to 1402

[4] Read Consociation Guidelines for Interrealm Treaties. Page 157.

[5] Read Yin's Volume VIII of Realm Studies Page 44 to 399

Haven

Visible indication is a white mist of a thick consistency reminding some observers of cotton candy.

Haven is a plane realm of breathable air, moisture in the form of clouds or mist, and no gravity. The ambient light is bright. No lifeforms or other identifying components have been found in the realm. [1][2][3]

Dwarves and Merfolk have often used Earth merely to experience the realm. [3][4] Other than the magic available by touching the realm, little of use exists there.

Hypothesises exist as to alternates states. [3][5][6]

Known bordering realms: Earth, Salmhalla, and Tarus.

(Cont. next page; Consociation Prohibitions)

[1]Read Yin's Volume III of Realm Studies. Pages 239 to 449 and appendix A

[2]Read Macrin's A Bridge to Haven; the Trail of Tears and Tribulations

[3]Read Innatala's Forgotten Path

[4]Read Soen's Research on Haven

[5]Read Ilionor's Mystics Realm

[6]Read Iai's Casual Observances and Lost Myths

Mer / Ishi-Iyai-Eyai-I

Visible indication is a blue-green liquid of a denser consistency than water.

Mer is a planet realm, a water-encased world with islands and some non-aquatic life. [1] Mer is the third planet from a hot star with higher than Earth surface temperatures and a single satellite. [2] Like Earth's humans, merfolk are the single indigenous intelligent life. Non-indigenous sentient life include the porpoises and whales, two of the numerous transplanted species between the two realms. [2]

No reported excursions into the realm have survived, and the merfolk refuse access to the realm, part of their reasoning for joining the Consociation.

Known bordering realms: Dur-Alf, Earth, and Tarus.

Interrealm travel from Earth by humans is prohibited by the Consociation Regulations. [4]

(Cont. next page; historical connection to Earth and Dur-Alf)

[1] Read Sienna's Treatise on Mer Isolation

[2] Read Tino Vangian Biography of Venis: Traitor of Mer

[6] Read Consociation Guidelines for Interrealm Treaties. Page 114.

Salmhalla

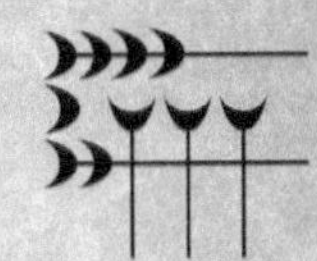

Indications include a liquid gold which is burning hot to the touch. [1]

Salmhalla is a plane of ambient sunlight and hot air temperatures. [1] [2] The plane contains a wide range of Earth-like terrains but predominantly includes mountains and grassy hills. [1] [2] [3] Several large water bodies have been detailed, but none rise to the level of oceans. [2] [3] [4] [5]

Consociation guidelines prohibit interaction with the realm and dragons enforce this edict. [6]

Known infringements have resulted in death, disappearance, mental illness, and loss of memory.

(Cont. next page; Known, theorized, and postulated magics connected to the Salmhalla realm)

[1] Read Yin's Volume IV of Realm Studies. Pages 1121 to 1349 and appendix C

[2] Read Inhai Du Anya's Scriptures of the High Dragons. Pages 89 to 97.

[3] Read Serjin's Testimonials

[4] Read Ilionor's Biography of Reshin. Pages 245 to 271.

[5] Read Wooley's Anectdotal Studies of Salmhalla

[6] Read Consociation Guidelines for Interrealm Treaties. Page 57.

Tarus

   Visible indications are a dark-gray color and a misty consistency with glittering elements akin pin head .
   Tarus is a plane realm with no ambient lighting and an oxygen-rich atmosphere. [1][2] Theories vary that the indigenous lifeforms have abilities to perceive lower frequency magnetic waves, have other senses, or solely rely on tactile and auditory senses. [2][3][4] Most grimoires record little of verifiable evidence, but specimens from the realm have been studied extensively by multiple races. [5][6] A rocky, waterless terrain is a commonly accepted description. [2][4]
   Known bordering realms: Earth, Haven, and Ya Keya.

(Cont. next page; Consociation Prohibitions)

[1] Read Yin's Volume II of Realm Studies. Pages 71 to 549 and appendix B

[2] Read Rasputin's Walks Among the Undead, the annotated version.

[3] Read Serjin's Agreements in Darkness

[4] Read Ilionor's Dedication

[5] Read Finyai's Tarus Biology

[6] Read Ted Dansworth's Research of Tarus Corporeal

Ya Keya

   Indications include a light gray mist which is moist to the touch.

   Considered the hunter's dream world, it is a plane of blue gray twilight according to numerous excursions including a Merfolk expedition led by Antre.[1] The plane contains a wide range of Earth-like terrains but predominantly includes forests, plains, and savannahs. No large water bodies have ever been detailed, but marshes and bogs were noted.[2]

   Continued interaction with the plane consistently results in a transmutation on a cellular level and the werewolf's bodily fluids become contagious.[3] Longevity and increased metabolic functions have been studied extensively.[4][5]

   Witches and Merfolk have lost all abilities to interact with the realms once transmutation has occurred.

(Cont. next page; Known Inhabitants of Ya Keya)

[1] Read Antre's paper on *To Ya Keya: Sacrifice and Betrayal*

[2] Read Yin's *Volume III of Realm Studies*

[3] Read Jayne Dunham's *Voyage Home*

[4] Read Kizurra's *History of Akkadian Werewolves - the Dawn*

[5] Read Demot's *Monograph* for an in-depth biological reference

ALSO BY KEVIN A DAVIS

Please head to my website and join my mailing list if you'd like to be kept up to date on this series or my other books.

DRC Files - An episodic paranormal procedural series

Book One: Atlanta's Guide to Cryptids

Book Two: Tallahassee's Manual on Arcane Artifacts

Book Three: Carolina's Handbook on Summoning

Book Four: New Orleans Register of Vampires

Book Five: Daytona Beach Directory of Covens

Khimmer Chronicles - contemporary fantasy with magic and cryptids in modern day Tallahassee, Florida

"A plucky protagonist who's still finding her way propels this fantasy adventure." Kirkus

https://www.kirkusreviews.com/book-reviews/kevin-a-davis/wights-wrath/

Wight's Wrath - Book One

Death's Contract - Book Two

Fate's Betrayal - Book Three

High Fae's Quest - Book Four

Friday's Fifth - Book Five

Nyx's Blade - The Origin Story

AngelSong Series - contemporary fantasy with fallen angels and angels in modern day Eugene, Oregon

Penumbra - Book One

Red Tempest - Book Two

Coerced - Book Three

Demons' Lair - Book Four

Infrared - Book Five

If you haven't read the Origin story of the **AngelSong** series, *Shattered Blood*, then download a free ebook or purchase the paperback or audible on Amazon.

Find out more

Website KevinArthurDavis.com

Facebook @KevinArthurDavis

KevinADavis on Instagram

KevinADavisUF on Twitter

ACKNOWLEDGMENTS

I'm always thankful for April's support and encouragement on this series. If you're looking forward to the more, you have her to thank.

Robyn Huss, my editor, works her own word magic, drawing from the realms with deep development and copy-edit. If you enjoyed Daytona Beach, it's largely due to her. If you're a writer, I encourage you to look at some of the opportunities she offers - http://www.hussediting.com/

Thanks to Heather Norris, avid reader, sacrifice in the first book of the DRC Files, and someone who gets excited when I write another.

The Fireside Group; Tim, Siena, Rosemary, Mark, Vail, Billy, and Katharine keep me challenged to do better in my writing. Gratefully, they let me brainstorm a lot of what I'm working on with them. Arrash and Michele from Jody Lynn Nye's DragonCon workshop keep me on task with the most intricate details . Dianne and Brett from Apex have been there for me.

I still miss David Farland's mentorship, and the easy way he encouraged writers. Please pick up one of his books and enjoy the magical words he endowed upon the world. Writers, study his lessons at Apex Writers.

Jody Lynn Nye's Dragoncon workshop will always be my go to suggestion for an in-person critique for any aspiring writers. Her insight is invaluable.

Another suggestion for new and developing writers is the Authors Workshop Track at JordanCon where guests, including writers, editors, and publishers, work with authors directly. I'm biased about this track.

Heather Norris and Benson Strickland have supported me so much with this series and more that they deserve a big Thanks as well.

Support creatives! The wonderful cover art is by MIBLart! Consider them for your next design.

Thank you, dear reader, for listening to my tales.